THE

CONTRACT

THE
CONTRACT

BY

Henry Carlisle

The Bobbs-Merrill Company

INDIANAPOLIS AND NEW YORK

All chapter epigraphs are from an undated edition of
Roget's Thesaurus, circa 1880.

The Bobbs-Merrill Company, Inc.
A Subsidiary of Howard W. Sams & Co., Inc., Publishers
Indianapolis • Kansas City • New York

For Olga

"There is a possibility of death, according to Freeman . . ."

(Henry Miller, letter to Anais Nin)

Table of Contents

ATHENS — 1

I SEE WARREN — 9

HOME — 17

SHAG — 27

TIMBERLINE — 37

THE MAN ON THE WALL — 49

THE HAWK CLUB — 65

THE CONTRACT — 83

A WARNING — 99

POST MORTEMS AND MRS. PEABODY — 107

I CALL ON MRS. PEABODY — 139

A FATEFUL DECISION — 149

THE MAGIC ISLAND — 155

CONTACTS — 167

ENTER LORD BOBBY — 179

A LETTER FROM SHAG — 187

AU CASINO — 195

A NIGHT DIP — 201

AT WARREN'S — 209

MORE CONTACTS — 227

AT MAMA TIA'S — 235

LORD BOBBY'S SECRET MISSION — 247

THE CARIBE COCKTAIL — 263

EPILOGUE — 287

ATHENS

601. NECESSITY.—*N.* involuntariness; instinct, blind impulse.

necessi-ty, -tation; obligation; compulsion &c. 744; subjection &c. 749; stern –, hard –, dire –, imperious –, inexorable –, iron –, adverse- -necessity, – fate; ἀνάγκη, what must be.

star, -s; planet, -s; astral influence; sky, Fates, *Parcæ,* Sisters three, book of fate; God's will, will of Heaven; wheel of Fortune, Ides of March, Hobson's choice.

Phr. it cannot be helped; there is no -help for, – helping- it; it -will, – must, – must needs- be, – be so, – have its way; the die is cast; *jacta est alea; che sarà sarà;* "it is written"; one's days are numbered, – fate is sealed; *Fata obstant; dis aliter visum.*

I REMEMBER standing in the shadow of the Parthenon looking up to the place Lord Elgin pried off the marbles when the stone fragment detached itself. It parted just above the frieze, where the ragged, honey-golden ledge met the blue Kodachrome sky and started falling in the general direction of Aunt Lavinia. There was no wind. The time was about eleven o'clock in the morning. Aunt Lavinia stood about twenty feet from me, five feet from the pediments of the Parthenon, holding a lavender sun parasol, her yellow Lawrence of Arabia turban tied under her solid chin, oversized mauve sunglasses, powder, wisteria print, oxfords. She was looking out over the white city to the bay where Onassis' motor yacht rode at anchor. In the hot, still air, traffic sounds below seemed far away; somewhere, nearer, in the old section of Athens called the Plaka, an accordion and a comically loose-lipped trumpet carried on some kind of fiesta which had been in progress since our arrival the day before. Our guide, Hector, exhausted from the

3

exertion of remembering a set speech in English about the Acropolis, was sitting thoughtfully on a block of Pentelic marble studying his hat. Just then some sense attuned to the old pile towering above us made him look up.

"Avery," Aunt Lavinia was saying, still looking at the yacht in the bay, "I think we should not tell Mr. Onassis we are in Athens."

The stone, which had seemed to hang in the air at first, now gathered speed and was traveling quite fast when it struck with a giant crack fifteen feet from Aunt Lavinia. Hector, miraculously, was now thirty feet from where he had been an instant earlier, his hands covering his head. When he saw that no more stones were falling, he began waving frantically with his hat.

Throughout, Aunt Lavinia, under the parasol, was admirable. Paying no attention to Hector, she looked at the stone, studying it. It is worth noting, by the way, that she did not then look up to where it had fallen from—she looked at me.

"Avery," she said, "what happened?"

"Souvenir of Athens," I said.

"I don't see anything funny. I might have been killed."

"True," I said. "I didn't mean to be funny."

Now, as I looked up at the immemorial stone, I analyzed my own response to the event and, after a moment's thought, found it cool, praiseworthy, American. I had certainly realized from the first moment that the stone would fall well clear of Aunt Lavinia, and therefore that a cry of warning might have made her move in the wrong direction, fatally. Or, had I attempted to rush at her and drag her out of the way (our positions relative to the point of impact would have made it necessary for me to rush up to her, reverse my momentum, and *pull* her away), she might easily have resisted, and the outcome would certainly have been awkward and possibly tragic. I had kept my head.

Hector, meanwhile, was asserting his manhood by throwing his hat on the ground.

"What do you suppose made it fall that way, Avery?" inquired my aunt.

"I don't know," I said. "Weather. Time. The British. The Turks. Sonic booms. Who knows?"

"Isn't it dangerous? Mightn't other stones fall?"

"Possibly. As a matter of fact, let's go over where Hector is. We'll be safer there, and also, I think it would make him feel better."

We started across the rough stone, Aunt Lavinia on my arm, parasol up, picking her way through the debris of antiquity, and I thought of what we must have looked like to Hector, even as he ventilated his great Athenian ego: Figures from a pageant called *The Decline and Fall of the United States*, the Rich American Widow and her Aging (I am thirty) Son—except, Dieu merci, I don't happen to be her son but her nephew. Aunt Lavinia has no children—a fact which becomes significant in the course of this narrative—indeed, she and I and my father are the only survivors of our precarious branch of Ashleys, which for five generations has trusted its dynastic luck to one or two members a generation. Hector, in the full sun, was sweaty and indignant. Why didn't we run when he warned us? Didn't we realize the danger? Were we desirous of meeting our deaths? Instead of the argument he doubtless expected Aunt Lavinia only replied, "I should think you people could keep it in better repair."

Yes.

I looked down to the foot of the Acropolis where our rented Humber gleamed in the Mediterranean sun. Everything was as it was. The car. The uniformed driver holding Kee-kee, my aunt's toy poodle. Onassis' yacht. The trumpet and the accordion were softly chasing each other like musical cats. We started down again, through a group of sturdy blond German youths climbing rapidly, making heroic efforts not to be heard breathing. Halfway down the rocky path, Aunt Lavinia paused and turned back to look at the Parthenon; she said (and I quote verbatim throughout):

"Look at it, Avery, only the Greeks could have built that. They had a marvelous sense of proportion, you know."

We took our places at the lunch table. The Hilton. The sun was glaring on the silver and white linen. Aromas worthy of Olympus filled the room but just then I found them suffocating. I put on my dark glasses and looked out the window at the pellucid swimming pool, watching a lovely young girl in a bikini rubbing oil into a silver-bronze industrialist. She saw me watching her and smiled a yes-I-am-real smile. Beyond the pool terrace, over the rooftops of the city, like a dream of peace—the Parthenon.

Aunt Lavinia took up her huge menu. I took up mine. Inside it was a picture of the Parthenon.

And suddenly, as swiftly as thoughts fly in Rosicrucian ads, I was seeing another illustration. Figure 8, a photograph of the Parthenon in my history text. The book was open on the broad arm of a school chair, the varnish of it engraved by anonymous Mongol pencils. Casita Encantada, my weird school. I remembered Old Piltdown (Shag Bronston's and my nickname for Dr. Thomas Pelton, our history teacher), cadaverous, worn down by generations of Boys, intense in his faded hound's-tooth jacket with leather elbow patches, still consumed by his strange need to teach people things that happened before they were born, saying, "The Greeks thought their gods— no TALKING, now!—played a direct role in their (HAAAARUMPH, HACK) lives . . . built temples to them all over Peloponnesia . . . the Parthenon to Athena . . . Delphic oracle . . . Destiny . . . (HAAARUMPH!) Furies . . . Fate . . . Stop that TALKING, Oliphant! Sit up, Bronston! Fate . . . You too, Ashley! Orestes . . . What did I just say? Tell the class what I just said, Oliphant!" And right out the window was the Wild West, rolling right up to the School: scrub oaks, manzanita, dry hills scored by fire trails . . . I dimly remembered, up a dry arroyo, overlooking the Homes of the Movie People and the great vacuity of the Mohave Desert, an oasis of pine and lichen-covered rock . . .

Aunt Lavinia was saying something. I looked up from

7

the menu just as a busboy was approaching her from behind with a black water pitcher.

Oliphant, I thought, where was he now? Then I remembered.

"You aren't listening, Avery," she said, pointing to the
cover of her menu, which was bound in rough cloth. "I
said the Queen had the people make this cloth by hand so
they won't lose their craftsmanship. What are you thinking about?"

"The island of Saint Sebastian," I said, playing a game
called Telling Aunt Lavinia the Truth. Nothing much
ever comes of it. She just said, "Yes, Dotty Rodney says
there's a very nice place there," and turned her attention
back to the handicrafted menu. The sound of ice water
hitting her glass was deafening. I read

POSEIDON'S CATCH
Around his Palace, Beneath the Sea!!
(*Please come to the Kitchen and point out your fantasies.*)

Our waiter arrived.

Aunt Lavinia had the "Les Enfants du Pirée Seafood
Platter." I had the "Poulet Sauté Venus."

That afternoon we flew out of Athens, homeward
bound with a stopover in Paris and thence over the Pole.

I don't believe in fatality, Greek or domestic, but I find
it hard to believe that ordinary laws of chance were oper-
ating when, three days later, at the San Francisco International Airport—after an interval of more than ten years—I
was to see Warren Oliphant.

I SEE

WARREN

913. [Maleficent being.] EVIL DOER.
—N. evil -doer, – worker; wrong doer
&c. 949; mischief maker, marplot;
oppressor, tyrant; firebrand, incendi-
ary, anarchist, destroyer, Vandal, icon-
oclast; communist; terrorist.

savage, brute, ruffian, barbarian,
semi-barbarian, caitiff, desperado;
Mo-hock, -hawk; bludgeon man, bully,
rough, dangerous classes, ugly cus-
tomer; thief &c. 792.

cockatrice, scorpion, hornet; viper,
adder; snake, – in the grass; serpent,
cobra, asp, rattlesnake, anaconda; can-
ker-, wire-worm; locust, Colorado
beetle; torpedo; bane &c. 668.

cannibal; Anthropophag-us, -ist;
bloodsucker, vampire, ogre, ghoul,
gorilla; vulture; gyr-, ger-falcon.

WE were 30,000 feet over frozen tundra, Paris behind us; the First Class stewardess (a Miss Bergstrom with catchy little å's and ø's in her voice) was setting up for the movie, the captain had just reported in that we were at mid-course and all was well.

"Avery," said Aunt Lavinia, who was beside me in the window seat, "can you think of a five-letter word with *r* in the third letter that means 'vivisection'?"

"No," I said.

She glanced up from the Paris *Herald*'s crossword (which she was "doing" with Kee-kee in her lap, looking on) and said, "By the way, I'm having a small dinner the day after tomorrow. There will be a young Sikh. I do hope you'll be home?"

"Yes," I said.

"You mean you won't?"

"No. I mean I will."

"I thought the way you said it you meant you didn't want to. Avery, is it Re the Sun God—or Ra?"

THE CONTRACT

Paris had been, needless to say, Aunt Lavinia's Paris: the Ritz (where she is known by the help as "celle-là"), Fouquet's, la Tour d'Argent, la Tour Eiffel, le Faubourg St. Honoré, Monsieur l'Antiquaire, le "gendarme" ("Aren't they helpful, Avery?"), la patisserie, l'ascenseur ("Oh, Avery, I haven't pushed anything and it's going up all by itself"), and a visit among my aunt's rare collection of dowager-pretenders to extinct monarchies, duchies, baronies; shrill women, mostly, living in dusty state in the George V district, serving tea under the family portraits; and of course Dior: I think of the young ashen-haired vicomtesse, petite, chic, mussable, with misty, witty eyes . . . I smile at Miss Bergstrom.

The cabin lights went off and the movie began. I got Aunt Lavinia's headset plugged in properly and turned up the volume for her. The film was called *Move Up to Murder*, and I soon abandoned my Parisian reveries and followed the intrigue developing on the screen. . . .

"Wasn't that amusing, Avery?" said Aunt Lavinia, when the film was over and the cabin lights went up. "I don't know how they ever manage to think up those stories. Do you?"

It was just an hour later when we were coming off the First Class ramp at the terminal that we ran squarely into Warren.

I had her hatbox. She had Kee-kee. Kee-kee was busy blinking at the people. Warren was coming off the ramp from another plane. He was followed closely by a blonde in a yellow mini-skirt who looked sleek, racée, and complicated, and five Negroes; to wit: a fierce, wiry old woman wearing what appeared to be last week's laundry and carrying a wooden box with wire-net apertures at either end containing an animal; a younger, big-boned woman dressed in cotton sacking; a stocky young man about my age with an intensely vague look; an old man; and another younger man carrying a tall, slender drum the shape of an enormous cigar stub. All the men wore clothes that looked as if they were ordered by mail and straw hats with rolled brims dashingly upswept in back. The man with the drum also wore glasses with mirrored surfaces. No one was saying anything: the girl and the five Negroes just followed Warren. Warren himself was wearing a British-cut suit that looked all the more British on Warren because Warren looks decidedly un-British. He has a cherubic moon face and remarkable eyes ringed with dark circles that make him appear as if he was permanently standing in an alley. The rest of his features are not individually remarkable, but the ensemble is unpleasant.

So there we were: Aunt Lavinia, me, Kee-kee and the hatbox on a collision course with Warren, the blonde, the five Negroes and the drum; however, at this point, Kee-kee took a careful look at Adrian and his group, stopped blinking, and barked.

"There, there, Keek-ums," said my aunt. "It's nothing, bun."

Simultaneously Warren looked our way, and the instant he recognized us, a grin split over his white teeth; unhesitatingly, he took the girl under her arm, increasing his

13

pace, and hurried her rag-doll fashion down the enclosed ramp toward the baggage area, the Negroes following Indian file.

Well, I don't think Aunt Lavinia noticed that Warren and the girl and the Negroes were a single party, for her remarks uttered a minute later referred only to the latter:

"They must be performers, Avery. One of them has a drum."

"Yes," I said.

"Look at those hats—they certainly aren't ours."

My aunt and I proceeded directly to the arrivals ramp outside, where Diedrich Kunzo, her half-Japanese, half-Filipino driver awaited beside the Bentley. It was a welcoming picture: the sun just nestling into the fog-streamers spilling over the coast hills, the Bentley vibrating with its fourteen coats of wine-dark paint, the lengthy ceremonial contortions of Kunzo's leathery face as we approached. I shoved the hatbox at him and went back in the terminal to claim our bags.

The five Negroes were standing in a tight group, watching the baggage appear, tip, and slide down onto the revolving distributor. The process seemed to absorb them. I couldn't find Warren but the blonde in the short yellow dress was standing not far from the Negroes, watching me. Then she started toward me through the crowd of waiting passengers, most of whom noticed her.

She had something to offend practically everyone, I thought admiringly: the humorous skirt, the tawny puss-in-boots boots she was wearing, youth (twenty or twenty-one, I guessed), a long-lined fausse-maigre figure, does-she-or-doesn't-she Montrachet-colored hair, and an expressionless face that was both worldly and doll-like, like an Oriental bar girl's, with wide-set blue eyes and thin, vaguely pouting lips.

"Greetings, Brother Ashley," said the lips. She was looking at me steadily but nothing else was working. Blank.

"Greetings—?"

"Shill."

"That's all?"

"That's enough," she said and handed me a little white card. "He said to give you this."

I took the card without looking at it.

"What is Warren these days?" I asked her, glancing at the Negroes. "Some sort of impresario?"

She laughed once. Hard.

"That's one name for it," she said, her expression immediately blanking out again. I looked at the card; it said

The Hawk Club
PRESENTS
"CARIBE COCKTAIL"
calypso—voodoo
limited engagement
topless waitresses

There was a phone number handwritten in ink on the bottom. I flipped the card over and looked at the back. It was blank. So was my mind at the moment.

"Call him at that number tomorrow. Around one," said Shill. "And he says if you come to the club, come alone."

I felt a prick of annoyance.

"Wait a minute," I objected. "I have no intention of seeing his show and perhaps it would be more convenient if he calls me. I'm staying at my aunt's just now. Mrs. Seward Vigorex, on Washington Street. The number is—"

"We know." For the first time, a trace of something showed in her face: cold, ironical amusement. It didn't last: "I suppose that's why he thinks you should call him. He also said when you come to the club, come alone."

My annoyance was now apparent, but I forced a laugh. "Do you mean Warren expects me to come to this—show of his, or whatever it is, and come alone? Well, please tell Warren that if he—"

"Remember the rules, Brother Ashley."

"Rules?" I said, noticing a couple of Medicare candidates staring at Shill and me with American Gothic expressions. "What rules?"

"The Contract," said Shill simply.

HOME

803. WEALTH.—*N*. wealth, riches, fortune, handsome fortune, opulence, affluence; good –, easy- circumstances; independence; competence &c. (*sufficiency*) 639; solvency.

provision, livelihood, maintenance; alimony, dowry; means, resources, substance; property &c. 780; command of money.

long –, full, –, well lined –, heavy- purse; purse of Fortunatus; *embarras de richesses*.

pelf, Mammon, lucre, filthy lucre; loaves and fishes.

rich –, moneyed –, warm- man; man of substance; capitalist, millionnaire, Nabob, Crœsus, Midas, Plutus, Dives, Timon of Athens; Timo-, Pluto-cracy; Danaë.

afford, well afford; command -money, – a sum; make both ends meet, hold one's head above water.

become -rich &c. *adj*.; fill one's -pocket &c. (*treasury*) 802; feather one's nest, make a fortune; make money &c. (*acquire*) 775.

enrich, imburse.

worship -Mammon, – the golden calf.

It is well known that rapid travel through several time zones is upsetting to our biological clocks and hence to our perspective of things. I was still on Paris time, and my watch, given to me by Aunt Lavinia in Mexico City a year earlier as a reward for Service and Fidelity, said 12:05, miércoles. The days are in Spanish. So, on the ride up the Bayshore Freeway to the city, I was able to accept my glimpse of Warren and the encounter with the girl called Shill as nothing more than a rather piquant Happening. My mind had been on getting the bags. As for "the Contract," I had at this time only the haziest notion of what it was: some infantile joke we had had back at school, Warren, Shag and I—involving our three aunts. (What did shock me, I remember, was that the *girl* should mention it.) As we Bentleyed past oversized motel signs and billboards advertising cheap air travel to Los Angeles, I felt the card in my pocket and reminded myself to think more about the incident at the airport when I was back on Pacific Standard Time.

THE CONTRACT

Offenbach or possibly Mozart would be the proper accompaniment to the ceremony of Aunt Lavinia's arrival home. Andante. Kunzo holds the car door. I hold Kee-kee. Aunt Lavinia gets out of the car and I hand out Kee-kee, get out myself and retrieve the hatbox from the front seat. Kunzo opens the iron outside gates and we enter the courtyard, a vast area of stone and masochistic shrubbery along brick walls on either side and under the brick Italianate façade of the house, with stone benches, terra cotta niches, a triumphant lead fountain, lead statues, stone statues, etc., etc. The main door opens as we approach it and Françoise, her tall, black West Indian butler, comes forward and inclines to her, I hand him the hatbox, the gates clang shut behind us. (Kunzo will now drive around the corner and down the hill into the service drive, where he will unload the luggage and carry it inside to the elevator in the pantry.) Bridget, Aunt Lavinia's personal maid, is standing by the main staircase. François hands her the hatbox. (On this occasion, there was a muffled scream from below stairs. In entering the pantry, Kunzo evidently frightened Cora-the-Cook, who startles easily.) Bridget starts upstairs with the hatbox, accompanied by the elevator full of luggage. Aunt Lavinia smothers Kee-kee in mink and says, "Isn't it too wonderful to be home, little button." Coda.

In the pantry (where Cora is now recovering herself) there is an old-fashioned, hardwood-framed, glassed indicator box, which tells the staff where to go when the buzzer buzzes. If you press all the buttons in the house (and pull the brocaded bell-pull in the living room), all the little brass indicators appear in the little squares:

Front dr.	Conserv.	Master bed	Master bath
Library	Living	Dining	Billiard
Up. Sitting	West bed	South bed 1	South bed 2
Ballroom	Sun Terrace	Loggia	Service dr.
Gate	Garage		

Since some of the events I will be relating take place here (and because the house has a certain interest for its own sake), I will very briefly describe its interior plan.

The lower floor is divided into two parts: the pantry, kitchen, laundry and servants' area and, across a long ogival corridor, the Conservatory and the seldom-used Ballroom (accessible by the main staircase). The Ballroom is larger but the Conservatory is the most bizarre feature of the house: a humid room full of jungle greenery in tubs, with north, perpetually steamed windows, in the center of which is a shallow sunken pool with a rock climb-out where Clarence, my late Uncle Seward's alligator, still lives at a great age, uncomplainingly.

THE CONTRACT

(For many years, an automatic tape system has been playing Everglade sounds continuously in the Conservatory, twenty-four hours a day. There are strident egret calls—I believe they are egret calls—chirps, bird songs, a few surprising screeches of God-knows-what, a heavy splash like one of Clarence's fellows bellyflopping into a swamp, assorted frogs, the drone of a light plane, and once in the three-minute cycle, a mud-sucking sound.)

On the main floor are the reception hall with its handsome staircase (and the main elevator cage), furnished in a massive baronial style with Louis XIII chairs, an Aubusson carpet, armor, torches, reflecting my uncle's feudal tastes. Beyond, past the staircase, is the entrance to the double living room, which extends the entire north, Bay-facing end of the house. On the left of the hall are the double doors to the dining room (accessible to the kitchen by a small service elevator); on the right, identical doors to the library; the billiard room beyond.

On the second floor are the master suite on the Bay side, the loggia, and on the south and west sides, the guest bedrooms. The south bedrooms (one of which is mine) face out over the courtyard and across the street into a block-square public park with green lawns, steep ivy-covered knolls, pines, cypress, well policed. The west bedroom looks over a brick wall to the equally imposing home of Aunt Lavinia's neighbor, Mrs. Floyd Rodney, who is also a widow. Below, seen from the Bay side windows, are the service court, four-car garage, chauffeur's quarters, tennis courts.

Leaving Aunt Lavinia in conference with François

about the dinner the following evening (the invitations for which, I found, had been issued by transatlantic telephone), I went up to my room. Among the mail on my desk, there were twelve invitations, ten of which were for cocktail parties, two for dinners before the Bachelors' Ball. There was a past-due bill from The Twin Peaks Speed Shop for a new electric fuel pump for my ancient Jag. Also a request from the Alumni Committee of the Casita Encantada School for Boys for money (". . . according to your pocketbook and interest in the School . . .") for the Building Program. Finally, there was my bank statement. Like a submarine commander, I tore open the envelope. It said $481.66. A quick calculation told me that with my current bills paid, I would be worth something under $300.00, except that there would be the expenses of dates, gas, tobacco, and my subscription to *The American Ballooner.* My glance fell on the framed (Kotzbeck) studio photograph (Harcourt) of Patricia Bunson on the desk; the picture made her look unflusterable and Junior Leaguey with a backlight livening her raven hair slightly. Above the portrait, on the wall, was another framed photograph: the Casita class of '54. I took it down and studied the adolescent likenesses of Shag, myself, and Warren, standing together in the back row. I was doing my best to look disenchanted, Shag was pulling his cheeks in to look thinner, but Warren—with his dark-circled eyes and little lemon-wedge smile—looked so unattractive that I wondered how Shag and I could ever have had anything to do with him. . .

Minutes later, in the privacy of the library, I called

23

Shag at his apartment; when his voice came on, I had to hold the phone away from my ear.

"You're back from the wars."

"We have returned."

"Want to talk about it?"

"It's too soon. But listen—"

"Did the Europeans all behave themselves?"

"They were wonderful. Very picturesque and helpful without being servile. Shag—"

"Did they say thank you for everything the United States is doing for them?"

"It got quite embarrassing. Look, I saw Warren."

There was quite a long pause on Shag's end. Finally, he said, "In Europe?"

"San Francisco. At the airport."

Another pause.

"With some Negroes and a girl," I added; but Shag did not respond to this information. Instead, he said,

"I thought he was supposed to be down in the Caribbean running guns or something. What's he doing up here?"

"Seems to be in show business."

"Good old Warren," said Shag. Then without advance warning, he guffawed. I held the phone farther away. "He didn't say anything about the Contract, did he?"

"Yes, as a matter of fact," I told him. "Indirectly, he did."

No answer. Somewhere out in Bell Systemland, I heard two women's faint voices chatting. Briefly, I described Warren's unusual behavior, my encounter with Shill, the card, the order to telephone him. "I don't even remember what the Contract was, exactly," I added.

Further silence. Then he said, "Free for lunch tomorrow?"

"Yes."

"Meet me at the Club at one."

I started to protest but stopped when I didn't hear the women's voices talking any more.

That night, after a light supper with Aunt Lavinia, I went up to my room. As I was closing the curtains, I saw Warren and another figure in the park across the street watching the house. They must have seen me in the window, for in the next second, they turned quickly back into the darkness behind a tree. In the instant before they disappeared, the street light showed the second man's hat: straw, upswept in back.

SHAG

626. PLAN.—*N*. plan, scheme, design, project; propos-al, -ition; suggestion; resolution, motion; precaution &c. (*provision*) 673; deep-laid &c. (*premeditated*) 611- plan &c.

intrigue, cabal, plot, conspiracy, complot, machination; under-, counter-plot.

schem-ist, -atist; strategist, machinator; projector, artist, promoter, designer &c. *v*.; conspirator; *intrigant* &c. (*cunning*) 702.

HERE used to be writers and artists in the Writers and Artists Club, but today the membership runs heavily to businessmen. Once a year they kiss their wives good-bye and gather in a glade north of the Bay where they entertain themselves with theatricals said to be "better than Broadway." Shag belongs; I do not.

Promptly at one, I arrived at the clubhouse, an austere brick building in downtown San Francisco, learned that Mr. Bronston had not come in yet, strolled into the main lounge (somber paneling, deep leather armchairs, portraits of Club Immortals, mooseheads, large table with bronze of a galloping cowboy swinging a lariat, newspapers, magazines) and took a *Wall Street Journal* for the form and settled into a chair to watch the ritual of the Western business community meeting for lunch.

Then—just as this spectacle was leading me into oppressive reflections on my temporary lack of a paying career —Shag was standing in the doorway looking for me.

Shag Bronston is a big, attuned guy who is professionally a junior partner in the law firm of Frobisher and

Sykes, specialists in estate management; socially the sole nephew of Mrs. Lorrillard (Christine) Peabody, one of the city's most prominent dowagers; politically a Republican; athletically a squash and tennis player (with an elemental sense of competition in every other game, from darts to dominoes); musically a guitar player with a large repertoire of loud songs, like "Men of Harlech" and "When the Roll Is Called Up Yonder"; and privately—let me say only that you would have to look hard for the reflective, haunted side of Shag. He is a realist, a practical man, and, though anything but a Marxist, believes firmly that life is based squarely on economics—Money. I have noticed, for instance, that when thinking, Shag usually stands with his hand in his wallet pocket.

We proceeded directly to the Tap Room where we took a table and Shag grabbed a waiter (literally) and we ordered vodka-martinis-on-the-rocks. The walls of the Tap Room are hung with more portraits of Club Immortals and more mooseheads. Behind the bar, there is a very large mural dulled by time and smoke to an art nouveau russet green, symbolizing The Marriage of Art and Commerce. Flanking this work are paintings done for posters of Club revelries. Our waiter headed off to the bar—along which, standing and sitting, the young San Francisco businessmen present were a silhouetted frieze under The Marriage of Art and Commerce. Our first exchange was merely ritual:

"How's Aunt Lavinia?"

"Sound as a dollar," I said. "Aunt Christine?"

"She goes on. It's amazing."

We looked at each other, dead-pan.

Then Shag said, "O.K. now, what's this about Warren? We wouldn't be pulling old Shag's leg, would we?"

I described exactly how I had seen our former schoolmate at the airport and what Shill had said to me, including her reference to the Contract. Just then something in Shag's manner stopped me from telling him about seeing Warren in the park.

"O.K.," he said, all Mr. District Attorney, "how much do you remember about the Contract?"

I tried to think.

I remembered the sun.

And then, again, I remembered Warren, Shag and I up in the pine-and-rock bower on the mountainside behind the School—Murietta Springs, it was called, our favorite hide-out and smoking place. It was hot; the "Springs" had no water and probably never had, except in some crazy prospector's dream; the Mohave Desert was one immense shimmering glare; around in the foothills were the long, low Homes of the Movie People, with swimming pools and palms; and below us, the aftermath of the Graduation Exercises: Punch and Cookies on Mudd Field. It was our last day together before "stepping off on the high road towards the Great Unknown," as Fogg the Headmaster had so unfortunately expressed it in his speech that morning, and I had inaugurated the Journey by falling dementedly in love with the sister of a Lower Schooler named Dimworth through a pair of salt-encrusted surplus binoculars which we ordinarily used for sniping quail.

"It was hot," I said.

"Go on."

I remembered the Parents and Friends of the School, the Faculty down on the field—and our three aunts together talking to Fogg.

"It was one of those wild ideas we used to get. Like kidnaping Fogg."

"Go on."

"We were going to get rid of aunts, weren't we? Or something like that." It began to come back. "For our inheritances, wasn't it? Some sort of a mutual arrangement?" Shag said nothing. "What were the stupid details?" I asked impatiently. "I have a sort of blank."

"And little wonder," he told me, "considering you were beautifully crocked on that rum we had, hypnotized, and on top of everything, violently infatuated with Dimworth's sister."

The waiter brought our drinks.

"I wasn't hypnotized," I protested. "I was sort of sunstruck. I don't think Warren really hypnotized me then, I just went along with it. I do remember Dimworth's sister, though." I had a vague but pleasant remembrance of a slim, virginal girl of seventeen or eighteen in a green dress and green beret.

"Boy," recalled Shag, "we were sure hard up in those days." Curtly I asked what Dimworth's sister had to do with the Contract.

"Only that that was how it all started," he said. "You were lying there on your stomach looking at Dimworth's sister through those glasses we had and you said, 'I would give anything in the world for that girl and Aunt Lavinia's money.' "

"I could *never* have said anything so idiotic."

"But you did. Then somebody yelled, 'Let's kill our aunts. Bang. Bang. Bang!' "

I remembered.

"That was you," I said.

Shag suddenly looked serious. "Maybe," he admitted, "but it was you who had the really great idea of us taking care of each other's aunts. Cheers." Shag raised his glass in tribute.

"Cheers. I thought it was Warren's idea."

"No, sir," said Shag, like a man who never mistakes his facts, "that was your brainstorm. Warren just got all worked up about it, but it was really your idea."

"Need I remind you I was jesting?"

"So was I."

"Warren can't be crazy," I said.

We took our second drinks into the main dining room, where a lot of young businessmen were lunching on Diet Specials and corporation politics. Shag greeted several acquaintances as we went to our table. We sat down. We ordered Small New York Cut Steaks. Just then, I wished I was in New York.

"How did we work it out exactly?" I asked. Shag, of course, remembered it all to the last detail.

I was to eliminate his Aunt Christine (the very thought of it caused a numb feeling in my wrists), Shag was re-

sponsible for Warren's Aunt Jane, and Warren was to
take care of Aunt Lavinia. We even wrote it down. I remembered that part of it.

"We wrote it down," I reminded him.

"Yes," said Shag, warming with School nostalgia, "the
guy whose aunt it was would have a perfect alibi. Rather
neat."

"I saw him in the park last night."

". . . and we had all those great ways of doing it, like—
Huh?"

"I saw him in the park last night, watching Aunt Lavinia's house. There was somebody with him." Shag
thought about this solemnly. Shag has a very expressive
face for a lawyer.

"I thought you said you saw him at the airport?"

"I did, but I saw him again in the park last night watching the house. Why would he be watching the house?"

Right then, we were two thoughtful San Franciscans,
Shag and I. After quite a while, Shag said, "There's really
only one thing that bothers me."

"What's that?"

"Warren hasn't been leading what you'd call a model
life since he left the School. That's what bothers me."

"I never believed all that," I said, recalling the rumors
we had heard some years before concerning our friend's
alleged activities in the Caribbean. According to one
story of a friend of Shag's (an Indian lawyer with the
State Department), Warren was known throughout the
West Indies as a man of undercover operations, some
lethal and all illegal. By this account (which Shag and I
had passed on with certain exaggerations we felt were

due our ex-companions' reputation), Warren was a professional gun runner, drug smuggler, blackmail artist, murder-for-hire broker—a sort of one-man Mafia.

"Let's for a moment assume the worst," he said, brightening, for like most lawyers Shag functions best when there is promise of disaster in a situation. "Let's go over the whole thing logically. For instance, all Warren must really want is to have Aunt June taken care of, for *his* inheritance. I'm speaking theoretically, of course. So obviously, he isn't going to do anything unless he's sure we will."

"And we won't obviously, theoretically. What's the matter?" Shag had stopped sawing his steak and put his knife and fork down. He looked suddenly unhappy.

"What did you say a minute ago?"

"About what?"

"About 'we wrote it down.' "

"We wrote it down."

I thought back. I had had a piece of binder paper in my pocket, a homework paper. We wrote the whole thing down on the back, with whereases and to wits, a solemn drunken oath, signatures in—yes—blood. Quail blood, but blood. We did it right.

"And he kept it," said Shag.

I objected that he wouldn't have kept the ridiculous thing all these years and that even if he had, it wouldn't have made any difference. But Lawyer Shag felt otherwise, I give him credit for that.

"Ave," he said, "if Warren's got that little document, he's got the proof all three of us were guilty of criminal conspiracy."

"But it was a joke!"

"Correct," agreed Shag with dogged reasonableness. "You know it was a joke, I know it was a joke, the only question is—does he?"

The waiter was watching us, bouncing in a most unwaiterlike way on the balls of his feet.

Through the rest of lunch, we went over and over the possibilities and finally convinced each other there was no immediate reason for panic. At worst, we decided, Warren was just playing around. We decided to call him and make it clear we weren't interested in juvenile games any more. That was our policy. It made us feel better.

I called from one of the pay phones just off the lobby; a man with a gravelly voice answered and I asked for Warren.

"Who wants him?"

I gave my name. Silence. A minute later, a girl's voice came on.

"Mr. Frog?"

"Shill? Someone must have made a mistake—I was asking for Warren."

"No mistake. Warren's asking for you. You and Mr. B. Tomorrow. 1406 Franklin Street. Nine in the evening. Got it?"

"Yes, but—" I found myself talking to the dial tone. When I told Shag what the girl had said, he recognized the address as Warren's Aunt June's.

36

TIMBERLINE

374. WOMAN.—*N.* woman, she, female, petticoat.

feminality, muliebrity. fair –, softer-sex; weaker vessel.

dame, madam, *madame,* mistress, Mrs., lady, *donna, belle,* matron, dowager, goody, gammer; good -woman, – wife; squaw; wife &c. (*marriage*) 903; matron-age, -hood.

nymph, wench, *grisette;* girl &c. (*youth*) 129.

[Female animal] hen, bitch, sow, doe, roe, mare; she-, Nanny-goat; ewe, cow; lioness, tigress; vixen.

gynecœum.

ODDLY enough, as soon as I left Shag in front of the Writers and Artists Club, I felt fine. I can't explain why. Perhaps the prospect of meeting Warren face to face—after his exotic behavior at the airport and his apparition in the park—reassured me somehow. Also, it was a nice day. Sunny, light wind, quite mild. So I decided to work on a play I was writing, the drafts of which happened to be at the vacant office of Horizons, Inc. (I will not detail the travel bureau phase of my career; the only significant facts are that the office was still held on a long lease and is located in a place called Ghiradelli Plaza.)

If you haven't been there, Ghiradelli Plaza is a chic casbah of shops, restaurants, cafes and terraces adjacent to the old brick Ghiradelli chocolate factory down by Fisherman's Wharf. The wind here is chocolate flavored. Young matrons from Pacific Heights come down to meet for shopping and lunch at Señor Pico's (while their husbands are at the Writers and Artists). The mannequins in the shop windows look like them, in their smartly cut suits and small hats. (In one window, there is even a Negro maid-mannequin in a black-and-white uniform serving little mannequin canapés.) It's all clean and well done and planted by good landscape people and there are the tourists and the young matrons and the junipers and azaleas in concrete planters and the Negro maid and the chic shops and the chocolate wind and the view of the Bay. Nice. Exactly the sort of place nothing happens.

And this is where I met Timberline.

I saw her name on a poster on an easel in the window of Freddie Van Deusen's art gallery, which is next door to Horizons, Inc. Pegasus West.

T I M B E
R L I N E
S T . D
E N I S ·
S C U L P
T U R E ·

it said. Next to the easel there was a piece of sculpture, a life-sized seated figure of a lumpy woman with her eyes closed, and dressed, as far as she was dressed, in cobwebs: sort of here and there: from her head to her shoulders, ankles to the ground. I should mention that my grasp of modern art is minimal. As I unlocked the door of Horizons, Inc., I reflected that Timberline was a rather unusual name.

Timberline

The travel posters were still up: Normandy, Greece, Rome, Jamaica, Haiti, Ireland, Holland, Saint Sebastian, Bern. The windows needed washing. I uncovered the IBM typewriter on the desk behind the counter and switched it on; it purred. At least the electricity hadn't been stopped. I sat down at the desk, found my manuscript in a drawer, put a sheet of paper in the IBM, and picked up the thread of my story.

Colin (hotly): But it's folly to stay here, sheer folly. Can't any of you see that?

Maureen (quietly sewing): Colin is right. The house slid again last night. It must have been the storm. We cannot stay here much longer, i' faith.

Hester (turning suddenly from the stove where she is making thin broth): Stop! Can't you see what you're doing to your father?

I had just gazed up to the poster of the green hills of Ireland for inspiration when the man from the Pacific Gas and Electric Company came in to shut off the electricity.

As the electric man went out, she walked in. I had no time to protest, even if I'd wanted to, which I didn't. She was wearing blue jeans spotted with plaster, a man's blue shirt with the shirttails out. Her great green eyes took in the empty office, the posters, then me. Her long hair was the color of old gold.

"Excuse me," she said, "do you have any glue?"

"Glue?"

"Yes, or mucilage; anything. I'm setting up my show next door and one of my cobwebs came off."

"I'm Avery Ashley," I said.

She smiled an if-we-must smile and looked at the desk. "Perhaps in one of those drawers there," she said.

I started opening drawers. "You say one of your cobwebs came off?"

Instead of answering, she inspected the room again.

"Are you a travel agency?"

"No," I explained. "I used to be a travel agency. Will this do?" I held up a card with two tubes under a plastic cover.

"What is it?"

"Epoxy." I looked at the directions. "Says it's just the thing for cobwebs." I handed her the card.

"Thanks," she said, taking it. "By the way, are you English?"

"No," I answered. "It's just that I go all to pieces when I meet a pretty girl."

Exactly an hour later, after I had helped her put the cobweb back on, we were out on the sea-wall at the beach watching the Pacific Ocean over foot-long hot dogs. I had learned she was from New York, that she lived with her parents in a loft apartment over a downtown warehouse, that she had met Freddie at a party in New York. She had accepted his offer of a show at Pegasus West because she had wanted to see California. In Golden Gate Park, I found that she had never seen a buffalo.

But it was only when we were sitting on the sea-wall, pegging pieces of bun up to the sea gulls, that I began to get a real idea of the kind of person Timberline was. I had asked her, conversationally, how she liked San Francisco.

"Well, the *city's* fine," she said.

"But the people?"

"Unbelievable."

"Thanks a lot."

"Oh, I didn't mean you," she quickly reassured me. "I mean some of those *society* people I met with Freddie. Some of the women in this town—"

"Unbelievable?"

She looked at me suspiciously and asked me what I was now that I wasn't a travel agency.

"British spy," I said, lighting my pipe against the wind. But Timberline insisted and I explained that professionally, at the moment, I was a statistic with the Department of Labor, that I was writing a play about Irish people, that I had a burning interest in sport ballooning, and that there was my aunt.

"Your aunt?"

"Yes, I have an aunt who takes a lot of looking after."

43

"She's sick?"

"No," I said. "Aunt Lavinia isn't sick. Not clinically. In fact, she's actually in very good shape. It's just that she needs a lot of looking after."

"What about your parents?"

I pointed out over the combers. "Out there," I said. "Pacifica."

Timberline asked me if they were dead.

"Oh, no," I explained. "My father lives in Tahiti. He's sort of a beachcomber in a way. My mother's remarried and she lives near Diamond Head. So they're out there but not together. I get letters from my father."

"And your mother?"

"And my mother."

"And this aunt you have to look after is—which?"

"My father's sister—but you'd never know it. They're completely different. And I don't really have to look after her, it's just that I sort of live at her house at the moment."

Timberline considered this, then asked me to tell her about my play.

I did. When I finished, all she said was, "Where does the son want to get away to?"

"Dublin," I said. "Why?"

She flung a piece of bun at the shyest gull. "No reason. Have you ever thought of leaving San Francisco?"

"Occasionally, as a matter of fact."

"Well, why don't you?"

"You mean—"

"Just go."

"Perhaps I will some day, but I can't right now."

44

"Why not?"

"There's a little problem."

"Your aunt, I'll bet."

"Yes. Somebody may be trying to kill her."

"Who?"

"Somebody."

I don't know quite why I said it, I just did. I must have felt something like: if you've got something bothering you, get it out. Also, there was something elemental about Timberline's curiosity. She was looking into the sun with her eyes closed.

"Aren't you imagining things?" she asked.

"It may be nothing," I agreed, adding: "On the other hand, it might be something."

I knew she knew I was looking at her, wondering what she would say, but she just smiled a little. She had a few freckles.

"You're a romantic, aren't you?" she said finally.

"A romantic!" I said. "That's the first time anyone's called me that!"

"I mean you like to believe things, like 'Somebody may be trying to kill my aunt.' This sun feels good." A long Vistavision wave was starting to break.

"Don't you believe in things?" I asked her, after it crashed. She opened her eyes and looked at me.

"Just real things," she said.

"Buffalo?"

She nodded. The wind was shifting her hair around.

"Who's this mysterious somebody who's trying to kill your aunt?" she teased.

"The Archfiend," I teased back. Neither of us was

45

paying much attention to what we were saying just then. Words didn't seem important, just waves.

"Tell me about this aunt of yours."

"Well, for one thing she's terribly rich."

"Of course," said Timberline, "and she lives in a palace with peacocks."

"An alligator," I corrected her.

"Do you have an uncle, too?"

"No," I said, "he died quite a few years ago, in a ballooning mishap."

Timberline laughed happily. I saw suddenly that she didn't believe in Aunt Lavinia.

"So when the Archfiend kills your aunt, you'll inherit all her money and the palace and the alligator?"

"No," I told her, "the alligator goes to Fleishacker Zoo."

Finally it got chilly. The sun had gone down behind a bank of haze and looked like a great Sunkist orange out there. On the way back to the little house on Telegraph Hill where Timberline was staying with a friend, I decided to drive by Aunt Lavinia's.

"That's where I live," I told her, looking at her for understanding. "That's where I have to go to a stupid dinner in about an hour." Timberline looked at the house.

"Of course," she said, amused, "it's just the perfect place for you."

I didn't insist. (As a matter of fact, it was refreshing to think of Aunt Lavinia as a figment of the imagination.)

46

And when I left her at the top of the wooden stairway leading down to her friend's house, I asked her if I could pick her up after dinner. I said I would show her some San Francisco night life.

"Won't your aunt mind?" she said playfully. Somewhere down on the Embarcadero, a switch engine nudged a line of squealing freight cars.

"To heck with her," I said.

THE MAN

ON THE WALL

---

909. THREAT.—*N.* threat, menace;
defiance &c. 715; abuse, minacity, in-
timidation; fulmination; commination
&c. (*curse*) 908; gathering clouds &c.
(*warning*) 668.

391

HERE were seven of us gathered in the living room for pre-dinner cocktails, a small group and not blue ribbon; just some of Aunt Lavinia's regulars plus the Sikh. We sat in a semicircle in front of the fire. Over the mantelpiece between two rare famille noir vases of the Sung dynasty from Gumps, my Uncle Seward, aloof and dignified in a blue blazer and red ascot, gazed out from the gold frame, over our heads to the Bay and the lights of Tiburon, in lifelike silence. Behind his floating white moustaches a balloon and a basket are painted, as if awaiting him, and for the first time I wondered if the artist intended the hot-air balloon as a symbol of Eternal Life.

Aunt Lavinia was sitting across from me in her velvet wing-back chair, listening to the Sikh. It seems a Pakistani Sikh is something rare. Sitting forward on her right, he was a narrow young man of twenty-three or -four, with a certain Eastern stardust which somehow affected me the wrong way. He was touring the United States on a Vespa, carrying a rucksack full of letters of introduction. It appeared that he had fallen in love with the great spaces of America.

I was puffing on my Kaywoodie, martini in hand, half-following his brave efforts to explain the 1947 partition of the Indian subcontinent to my aunt, thinking of Timberline.

"That's all so fascinating, Mr. Kahn," she said when he finished. "And can you tell us whether there are dolphins in the Indian Ocean?"

The Sikh's smile came partly unfastened.

"Dolphins?" he faltered.

Next to the Sikh, deep in one end of a long pale gold sofa facing the fire, was Mrs. Reginald Pringle, widow. Her face at this time showed calm approval, for while Mrs. Pringle does not hear well, she is able to tell from the vibrations in a room whether anything is wrong. In her lap, her pre-World War II hearing aid was mimicking the Sikh's voice like a naughty child. At the other end of the sofa, sitting erect, was Mrs. Everett Bush, another widow, trying not to let herself be distracted by the electronic voice while following the Sikh's actual words carefully. Next to Mrs. Bush in a large armchair sat Witter Hill, also watching the Sikh (the featured novelty of the evening) interestedly. At sixty, Witter is a professional courtier to the dowagers of San Francisco: extra man, house guest, confidant, social historian, arbiter, counselor, secret agent, astrologer, numerologist, and, once a year, Cotillion Master. His full round face (Witter resembles a relative, perhaps the brother of a Roman Emperor) was solemn; he was leaning a little away from the woman on his right. This was Mrs. William Stockbacker, who with a mammoth bourbon in her hand was watching the Sikh with hostile curiosity, her eyes narrowed by smoke from a Camel stub in the corner of her mouth. She was wearing a silk suit with an aggressive horticultural pattern, and a cerise scarf fastened with a silver cow skull. With her fierce white hair, her honest, original Western face, she exemplifies California's special brand of weather-beaten independence. Mrs. Stockbacker has extensive ranch holdings and commercial property in Northern California. She is a widow and a Republican.

"You see, Mr. Kahn," assisted Aunt Lavinia, "I have read that they now believe dolphins capable of communicating with each other almost like human beings. Do you Indians believe that?"·

"Pakistani, Madame," said the Sikh, closing his eyes briefly. "Yes, it seems quite possible."

Bridget entered with a tray of hot crab canapés. Though Bridget is Irish, Aunt Lavinia dresses her like a French doll. That evening, she wore a lustrous black froufrou uniform with a tiny white apron tied in back with a gigantic bow, and a pert little starched cap atop her bog-colored hair.

"Birds communicate!" announced the Sikh suddenly, as if he had made a discovery.

"Well, of course they do!" agreed Aunt Lavinia, pleased that the Sikh was getting into the spirit of the conversation. She turned triumphantly to me, implying either that I disagreed with this secret of nature or that I should have mentioned it myself. I couldn't tell which.

53

I took my pipe out of my mouth, replaced it again and puffed.

"Of course," remarked Witter to the fire after a moment, "there's nothing very surprising about dolphins communicating when you think that certain human beings can sometimes communicate with each other thousands of miles apart." Mrs. Stockbacker snorted as I've noticed she does whenever the subject of the supernatural comes up.

In the dark, stately dining room, candlelight shone in the silver and crystal, and as we ate our turtle soup, the conversation turned to Negroes and robberies.

"I believe," Witter was saying, in what was for him an unusual burst of liberalism, "that the criminal element of ANY race should be made incapable of reproducing itself. I can't help it."

"It's our own fault for letting them get where they are," said Mrs. Bush. "That's what Ev always used to say."

"Put your money in a good stud horse," remarked Mrs. Stockbacker, apparently thinking of some past incident, "then let some darky try to steal it—it'll kick his head off."

Witter looked distressed, as if this remark had thrown his own thoughtful observation into an improper light. Mrs. Bush was now glancing apprehensively at the Sikh, as if suddenly wondering whether Sikhs were Negroes or Part Negroes; Mrs. Stockbacker ate her soup.

As the sherry was being served, everyone was silent, then Aunt Lavinia said to the Sikh, "Mr. Kahn, we were talking about a friend of mine who is the aunt of a good friend of Avery's, Christine Peabody. You see, she was burglarized last week—oh, it's happened often before—she has many fine things in her apartment—but this time, the burglar came right into her bedroom. What did the papers call him, Avery?"

"The Bat Burglar," I said.

"The papers always find some name like that," observed Mrs. Bush.

"And do you know," continued Aunt Lavinia, "he already had a big bag of her things, and she made this Bat Burglar turn them all right out on the floor. She *told* him what he could take and what he couldn't. She told him, 'If you must rob me, at least do it properly.'"

"Amazing!" said the Sikh. "But I don't see quite how she accomplished it, under the circumstances."

"Character!" put in Witter, ploughing a ladle of sherry into his soup. "Christine Peabody is a very unusual person."

"Her husband was a very well-known banker," said Mrs. Bush to the Sikh, by way of adding a footnote to his education.

"Christine is a dear person. I'm devoted to her," said Aunt Lavinia rather stiffly. Mrs. Pringle indicated by mute overtures that she was going to say something. Everyone listened.

"There's so much—violence—in the papers," she announced. Aunt Lavinia and Mrs. Bush expressed their agreement, and Mrs. Pringle, heiress to a California cement fortune, nodded until her emotions subsided.

"Yes, and Mr. Kahn," said my aunt, "we practically have a South American revolution right next door to us."

"Really?"

"Yes. You see, my neighbor, Dotty Rodney, has rented her house to an exiled general—of what country is he, Avery? Guatemala?"

"No," I said.

"—while she is visiting friends in England. Well, of course, the general's government is in exile on account of the Communists. Dotty says he's quite attractive though somewhat terse in English." Aunt Lavinia looked at the Sikh as if she was experimentally seating the general in his place at the table. "Now François tells me his house people say he has had threatening phone calls from political enemies, right next door to us."

"Oh, Lavinia," said Mrs. Bush, "we're hardly safe in our beds!"

Mrs. Stockbacker looked up from her soup and glared at Witter. "Perhaps not," she said, "but we're as safe there as anywhere else!"

Mrs. Bush laughed nervously and Aunt Lavinia said, "Oh, Daphne, I do think that's rather funny." (It is worth noting that when amused Aunt Lavinia does not smile or laugh but announces the fact in the form of a communiqué.) Witter shut his eyes.

"I told Dorothy not to rent to him," he said at last. "It's not safe for you, Lavinia. You know the South Americans yourself. You've been there."

"Why, Witter, you certainly don't think *I'm* in any danger, do you?" The wall slid open and François advanced from the elevator with a silver platter of sliced roast beef on which he had left the carving knife. Witter said nothing.

"Is it my horoscope, Witter?"

"Nonsense, Lavinia!" scoffed Mrs. Stockbacker. "Horoscope! I say if something's going to happen to you, it will, and if it's not, it won't."

"Precisely," said Witter.

"So why diddle with horoscopes?" fired back Mrs. Stockbacker.

With serene timing, Witter said, "I can't imagine living for *one minute* in a world without some purpose and order. I simply can't and that's all there is to it."

From the kitchen a floor below I heard the bell Aunt Lavinia was pushing with her foot. I thought of Timberline, but to my amazement I couldn't remember her face exactly.

Two or three minutes later, François reappeared in the elevator with Cora's Lemon Thing.

Up to now it had been a fairly typical evening at Aunt Lavinia's, and as usual, I felt a great need of fresh air. So, while my aunt and her guests drifted into the living room, I went to one of the French windows that open onto little stone balconies all around the main floor of the house, and reached for the switch in the casement that disarms the burglar alarm.

Then I saw the man on the wall.

THE CONTRACT

I could see him clearly, because from the dining room he was silhouetted against the glow of sodium vapor lights from the Golden Gate Bridge; he was sitting motionless about ten feet from the end of the high brick wall separating Aunt Lavinia's garden from Mrs. Rodney's. I froze. Though he faced our side, he hadn't seen me, because just then he was too busy peering into the living-room windows, where the company was taking places around the fireplace again, for Sanka. Faint music, upbeat tico-tico Latin rhythms, was coming over the wall. In the first moments, I simply watched the man without any particular feeling other than surprise. Then I recognized his rakish straw hat.

The man had half-turned and was now looking over his shoulder toward the Rodney house, and I saw that it was the Negro who had been carrying the drum. I was sure too that it was the man I had seen in the park with Warren. I watched as he stood up on the wall, turned, wavered slightly, then steadied himself, took something from his pocket which I thought at first was an apple because he bit into it and then tossed it casually into Mrs. Rodney's rose garden, under the living-room windows. It wasn't an apple. A couple of tico-tico measures later there was a pretty good explosion in the rose garden, the sound of shattering glass, then a long moment of silence. The man seemed to have disappeared. Then I saw that he had been lying flat along the wall as the "apple" had gone off, because now he got up to a crouch and started scrambling along the wall in the direction of the street. There was a commotion on the other side of the wall now, Latin shouts, the music suddenly louder and brassier as doors and windows were thrown open. I opened the French doors and stepped out on the balcony. Immediately, below and around the corner of the house in the service area, a great clanging started. The burglar alarm—I had forgotten to pacify it before opening the window. Below, I heard Cora scream, then a monumental sliding crash of crockery. The apple-thrower had almost reached the end of the wall when two rapid shots sounded. Like party snappers. More shouts in Spanish. I had the impression the whole thing was happening to the beat of the music. Two more shots. The intruder dropped off the end of the wall, safely, for a few seconds later I saw him running into the park. Someone turned the music off. The bell continued to ring. Aunt Lavinia appeared in the doorway and said, "Avery, didn't we hear something?"

As Witter came up beside her, looking distressed and officious, she added, "And isn't that our burglar system? That's the same noise it makes when the man comes to push the test button." I stepped back into the room.

"There was a man on the wall," I explained. "He threw a hand grenade or something under the general's window. There was also a little shooting."

"I hate to say I told you so," said Witter. Mrs. Stockbacker appeared in the doorway beside him and asked if it was a colored man. I assured her it was.

"What is it?" Mrs. Pringle called in a frightened voice from the living room.

"Shots, dear," shouted Mrs. Stockbacker. "Colored people."

"The police will be here, thank heaven," said Aunt Lavinia (referring to the fact that the burglar alarm automatically triggers an identifying signal on the police switchboard when it rings at the house). "They'll investigate. But, Avery, shouldn't you have simply telephoned them instead of tripping the alarm?"

Five minutes later, through the open French doors we heard the expiring growl of a police siren. The car's radio was turned up loud; I could hear it blaring out the evening's misdemeanors and crimes. The front doorbell rang downstairs in the pantry.

I guess I expected a police inspector to look like anything but a police inspector, so Inspector Ferguson surprised me. Through the doors to the hall I watched him handing his hat to François. He was slightly taller than average, of middle build, about fifty or fifty-five, gray suit, gray hair, and the same stalwart look of an inspector in a Margaret Rutherford film but without the British class sense.

"Oh, Inspector," said Aunt Lavinia, sweeping into the hall to meet him, "we're all so relieved you've come."

From the first, he seemed to be playing a deliberate game with me. Perhaps it was my imagination but I doubt it. Among all those present, I was the one Ferguson treated as a person of particular fascination. He adopted a sort of mock-respectful, bantering tone, and nothing I could say—or fail to say—eluded his attention. Of course I was the eyewitness, I had seen the man on the wall, but Ferguson's interest in me seemed to extend far beyond the prosaic facts I was telling him.

I suppose I might have been talking in unnecessary detail. I remember being annoyed that the more I tried to appear as an accurate, responsible, above-average observer, the more he persisted in seeing me as a curiosity. He would stare at me, just look at me calmly and carefully as if he was reading a water meter.

"—and so," I wound up at last, "I would say that it must have been about four or at most six minutes, from the time the man ran into the park and the time you got here in the police car."

Ferguson looked at me, waiting until he was sure I was through talking, then he said, "I didn't get here in the 'police car.'"

Now he was watching me as if I was some kind of chemical experiment in which something was supposed to boil.

Finally he said, "I came in a blue Chevvy. The two men who came in that car you saw are next door at the general's." He turned briefly to Aunt Lavinia to accept, instinctively, her silent applause; then he looked back at me.

"I didn't see the police car," I told him.

This unlooked-for response of mine seemed to delight the inspector.

"Ah, touché!" he said. "Of course you didn't see the police car from that window. You just *heard* the police car. Yes? Of course. But now about the man on the wall: you did see him—just as you've told us?"

"Yes, I saw him faintly, in the dark."

"And did you recognize him in the dark, Mr. Ashley?" He must have caught my hesitation, for he added, "I mean—put it another way—was it anyone you'd ever seen before?"

"No," I said. Too fast! I felt my blood throb; if I'd been taking a lie detector test, I would have knocked the stylus off the paper. He looked at me a long time (it seemed), then, incredibly, turned to my aunt and began explaining to her that the person I had seen was without any doubt a political enemy of the general's, or perhaps a hired assassin. The general had been threatened by telephone. He was leaving a man to watch the general—Aunt Lavinia, he was saying in effect, was in no danger!

Was his first behavior toward me, I wondered, without significance? I felt at once relieved—and then suddenly more anxious than ever as I saw him start back toward the front door.

"Shouldn't you leave a man here, too?" I heard myself asking.

Inspector Ferguson turned to me with the shanks of his teeth showing in amusement.

"Why, Ashley? I just said your aunt is in no particular danger."

"I'm sure I'm perfectly safe, Avery," co-operated Aunt Lavinia.

"Think I'm wrong about that?"

"Just as a precaution," I said lamely.

Ferguson said to my aunt, "You seem to be well looked after by this young man here. Kurdistan?" He was looking at a rug in the hall.

"Yes," said Aunt Lavinia. "They tell me it's a very good one. You must know Oriental rugs, Inspector?"

"Oh, I know a few things," he said, looking back at me again. "Mostly, I guess, I don't seem to ever forget anything." Then: "Good night, m'am. Sorry to have troubled you."

"No trouble, Inspector. Good night and—thank you."

François held the door for him and Ferguson disappeared into the night.

"Oh, Avery," said my aunt as we returned to the living room, "what an intelligent man!"

THE

HAWK CLUB

Adj.* vicious, sinful, sinning &c. *v.*;
wicked, iniquitous, immoral, unrigh-
teous, wrong, criminal; naughty,

unprincipled, lawless, disorderly,
contra bonos mores, indecorous, un-
seemly, improper; dissolute, recreant;
reprehensible, blameworthy, uncom-
mendable; dis-creditable, -reputable.

base, sinister, scurvy, foul, gross,
vile, black, grave, facinorous, feloni-
ous, nefarious, shameful, scandalous,
infamous.

Adv. wrong; sinfully &c. *adj.* without excuse.

Int. O tempora O mores!

AM attempting to write this as it happened at the time, without trying to justify myself or anyone else or explain anything I didn't understand at the time it was happening; but I will admit that at this juncture (after the inspector left), my own behavior is a puzzle to me. I wonder, for instance, why I didn't call Shag then; the thought never entered my mind. And wild as it may sound, my seeing the man on the wall—*and even my recognition of him as one of Warren's troupe*—still did not add up to positive proof for me that Warren was in earnest about the Contract. The man (I reasoned) had, after all, thrown the grenade under the general's window, not Aunt Lavinia's, and it was the general who had received the threatening phone calls. The theory that the man on the wall was actually trying to assassinate the general seemed logical and satisfactory; what was more, since Inspector Ferguson seemed to accept it, it was also official. Still, "just as a precaution"—in a spirit of exploration—I had decided to go to the Hawk Club that very night and confront Warren. I would see him with Timberline along; not alone, as Warren had directed, but on my terms. I felt quite exhilarated by this ridiculous decision.

After doing a lot of fussing over her, Aunt Lavinia's guests finally left. Witter declared he meant to walk all the way back to his flat alone. However, when my aunt ordered the Bentley to return the Sikh to his hotel, Witter was persuaded to relent and climbed in too. Mrs. Pringle's Cadillac and driver were waiting for her at the curb just outside the gates. Mrs. Bush drove her own Chrysler. Mrs. Stockbacker, I noticed, had come in a dusty Lincoln Continental with an ancient Goldwater sticker still on and a stock saddle in the back seat.

About quarter of ten, Aunt Lavinia and I fed Clarence (a ritual with semimystical overtones which I may have occasion to describe later), after which she retired and I went to the garage, climbed into my once-noble Jag, turned on the ignition, listened for the electric fuel pump, pressed the starter button and drove over to Telegraph Hill to pick up Timberline.

Her friend's house was the last one before the Hill falls off in a sheer cliff that drops to the Embarcadero. It was tiny and "bohemian." I knocked. From somewhere upstairs, Timberline called to me to come in.

In the downstairs room (a little kitchen adjoined it), there was a big studio couch, a rough wooden table with candles set in Cointreau bottles, a hi-fi, a few books and records collapsing in pine-board shelves, cushions on the floor, Mexican glassware, dusty Woolworth philodendrons. When Timberline came downstairs, she looked quite different from the girl I had been with at the beach. She wore a short, swingy ice-green dress and was quite beautiful, but different; the dressed-up Timberline seemed to present a whole trunkful of new mysteries. We both were a little embarrassed, as if we hadn't spent most of the afternoon together. She said, "I hope your aunt is all right," and I smiled at the joke and said, "In the pink." Then I remember her taking a pink coat from a closet that seemed to be full of costumes and masks.

"Where are we going?" she asked.

"To see the Archfiend," I said.

The first show at the Hawk Club doesn't begin until almost eleven, so we strolled down the Broadway Strip seeing the sights like a couple of tourists. The big word here is TOPLESS. We passed a theater advertising TOPLESS FILMS, two TOPLESS restaurants, an AMATEUR TOPLESS place, a bar offering a TOPLESS MOTHER OF EIGHT, and the place where Carol Doda, the ORIGINAL TOPLESS ATTRACTION, was dancing. We caught a glimpse of her inside, doing the Swim dressed in nothing but colored lights flashing to the tempo of blaring music. The big bouncer at the door looked as if he was permanently waiting for the police.

A few doors down, some people were filing into a club called El Matador. I looked at my Spanish watch. It was still fifteen minutes until show time at the Hawk Club, so we followed them in. None other than Barnaby Conrad himself greeted us. Our Host. I introduced Timberline, and Barnaby took us to a table and sat with us. Timberline admired his bullfighting pictures around the room, and when I told him about Timberline's show at Freddie's, they spoke of galleries and artists they knew in New York, and I sat back listening, smoking my favorite Kaywoodie, enjoying myself, until Patricia Bunson came in the door.

She was with a person I can't stand called Gordon Prescott-Peel, and two other couples. She was wearing a sport mink. Gordon towered beside her, looking around the room with his Seeing-Who-Was-There look. Pat spotted me immediately, but was looking at Timberline. She was smiling but didn't seem amused. The other two couples piled up behind them. One of the other girls was a big blonde called Whoopie who is so rich she permanently shrieks with laughter. Gordon Prescott-Peel saw me; he mock-waved and nudged Patricia, who nodded and said something to him which made him laugh; he whispered something to her and she shook her head; then they strung out in a file, Gordon in the lead, Whoopie's escort in the rear, Whoopie shrieking, and took a table; Pat sat down with her back to us.

A few minutes later Barnaby left us. As he got up, he promised to see Timberline's show and then said to me:

"Say hello to Lavinia for me. How is she, by the way?"

"Keeping fit," I said.

"You do have an aunt," said Timberline when he had gone.

"I told you."

"I mean you have an aunt who really lives in that enormous house. And you really live there too."

"Only for the present."

She thought a moment.

"And there is an alligator?"

"Clarence," I told her. "Now maybe you'll believe she's really in danger from the Archfiend?"

"No," she said, looking with disapproval at the table where Whoopie was shrieking at something Gordon had said. "But you know those people who came in, that girl, for instance."

"Yes. Acquaintances."

"Avery?"

"Yes?"

"Why did you tell me your father was 'sort of a beachcomber' this afternoon?"

"Well," I said, "I told you that because he sort of walks along the beach out there in Tahiti and picks things up. Later, he sells them to tourists in his little store. I'm what's called a poor relation."

"And that girl?" she asked, still looking at Pat and the others. "What does she do?"

"Do? Pat? She swims, sails, rides, plays tennis, and goes to lots of parties. She is a member of the Junior League and all kinds of benefit committees. Also the Spinsters. She studied piano and plays rather well. And every Tuesday she has lunch at the St. Francis Hotel."

"And she doesn't do anything?"

"No."

"And that tall man with her?"

71

"Gordon? You mean what does he do? He just sort of —turns up. I guess he has to talk to his broker now and then, though." I felt a mixture of sentiments just then: on one hand, Timberline's mistrust of San Francisco Society pleased me, on the other hand it didn't. She seemed to be condemning everyone just because they didn't "do" anything, and she seemed to be mixing *them* up with *me*. She watched the table critically, then turned to me again and in a faraway voice I hadn't heard before said, "Tell me about your uncle." We looked in each other's eyes and, as it had happened at the beach, were suddenly held there. "I didn't mean to laugh then," she said. "Only, from the way you talked, I didn't think you really had an uncle who—"

"—fell in a balloon."

"Yes. What was he like?"

"Sir Thomas Lipton," I said, noticing that her lips were part of her distinctive fascinations, "and almost as distant. He only liked to talk about business; the rest of the time he sort of grunted around. But he was a wonderful man, not at all like—what you'd expect. He took me up in his balloon once. I must have been ten or eleven. I never forgot it. The silence up there. No engine noise, you know. We could see half of California, from the Sierras to the Pacific almost. It was wonderful."

I wondered if Timberline had understood—she seemed to have her mind on something else, though she was looking at me steadily—and then I thought of New York. Fifth Avenue. The Verrazano-Narrows Bridge. Greenwich Village. Timberline's warehouse. Of course there

72

would be no ballooning in New York. That was the catch. But there was Long Island. Surely there would be open spaces, meadows, ploughed fields (excellent for thermals) on Long Island. The hazard would be the sea—going down in it. On the other hand, Long Island was probably bigger than it looked on the map, and much would depend on the prevailing winds. I saw us: Timberline in the basket with me, fixing little sandwiches, a scarf around her hair, the skyline of Manhattan in the distance.

"What did your uncle do to have all that money?" she was asking me.

"Cartels," I murmured.

I was already slightly familiar with the Hawk Club. I recognized the owner, who is Cy Ferrone, 250 pounds of unaffable muscle who keeps the town's columnists hopping to their dictionaries for new ways to say thug. Ferrone sports silk suits, black shirts, white silk ties, heavy cologne and books good acts usually: the sickest comics, the twangiest folk-rock groups; but in between the bigger draws he goes in for exotic specialty acts like Warren's "Caribe Cocktail."

The acts are only part of the appeal. In the first place, the waitresses are topless; however, the gimmick that sets the place apart from other Broadway Strip grottoes is the highly convincing True Crime atmosphere it exudes. According to the columnists' hints and what you hear around San Francisco, the Hawk Club is supposed to be a

73

sort of YMCA for Mafia dignitaries and their "button men," a place where real contracts are made and other nasty transactions arranged.

So, naturally, a couple of years ago when Cy took over the place, all the bright young-old generation of Pacific Heights jammed in to hobnob with the gangsters, just like the ones in the 'Thirties when they were kids. The idea of sitting next to a Tahoe gambling operator, a real loan shark, or maybe even a Mafia caporegime out from the East was pretty appealing. Post-debs and young marrieds loved the funny bartender and the funny waiter-bouncer, who were both big, sleek and heavy-weight and who looked exactly like the Boss, except that they were coatless, wore rubber bands around their shirt sleeves and reeked of Mennen instead of 1147. They got to know them by name. Gus and Louie. Gus and Louie were cute. And everyone knew Cy by sight and he was cute. Just a little grumpy. The topless waitresses ("poor things") were cute. For a whole winter season, "The Hawk" was the after-hour place to go, and then quite suddenly it wasn't.

In a few months, Society found that the Underworld was as dull as anything else one was outside of. Cy and his look-alike boys and the ranker element of the clientele were all so full of their hush-hush private affairs that they hardly noticed them. They wouldn't tease with them or get to know their names or take reservations for the best tables or even pretend they mattered at all. There was no intercourse. Projects to invite Cy to Pacific Heights cocktail parties were dropped. The Experience had been a failure. Once you've seen one caporegime you've seen them all, so suddenly everyone agreed that The Hawk was dull and *out* and the people there sordid and the whole place very boring. No doubt Cy was delighted to see Pacific Heights go.

Anyway, he had no trouble filling up the tables. When Timberline and I arrived, the place was almost filled with the sort of people Pat called "nobody," sitting around in the clinky darkness watching the voodoo dancers. They were performing on a slightly raised stage, reddish-lit, which occupied the back of the narrow room. The tempo of the drum and the dancers' sedate epilepsy indicated that the ceremony was nearing some kind of barbaric finish. Near us, on our right as we waited for Gus to show us to a table, Cy stood immobile behind the bar, staring at the cash register. At his right, Louis was expertly slopping liquor from balltop bottles into rows of glasses full of ice cubes, while across the end of the bar from him a redhead with a face like the Girl Next Door and breasts like the tops of fireplugs was waiting for her drink order. Gus, the other of Cy's sunshine twins, loomed from the obscurity and ice-broke a path for us among the tables to a cranny near the stage, took our order and disappeared again.

The dancers and the drummer were the same five I had seen at the airport—and I fixed my attention on the drummer, who sat on a stool with his knees supporting the tall drum which he beat alternately with the flats of his

75

hands and his fingertips. He was a young man with a circular, vacant face, and he was staring over the heads of the audience as if he was looking into some jungle night. I recognized him as the man on the wall. The faces of all five were eerily whitened with some kind of powder.

Timberline and I watched as the four dancers shuffled, rocked and rotated in an apparently random way, until you saw that they were moving around a center, but not really. For no visible reason, two would join hands and dance together, never, though, according to any satisfying pattern. They were chanting.

> Eh! Eh! Bomba. Eh! Eh!
> Canga bafɔ te,
> Canga moune de le
> Canga do ki la
> Canga li

Then, as my eyes grew accustomed to the reddish light, I saw Warren.

He was sitting at a table near the stage across the room from ours, looking at me; and when he saw I had seen him, a slow citric smile spread over his face and his eyes fixed on me like lasers. The girl Shill was next to him, also looking at me, but languidly, though when our glances crossed she smiled ironically, almost challengingly, as she had done at the airport. She wore a silvery metallic dress, amusingly low-cut. Timberline noticed her too.

The drum was beating faster. The climax was approaching. The old woman was doing a kind of tango with a white chicken she had produced from somewhere. The young male dancer was drawing something on the floor with a trail of meal from his hand.

"Who is that girl?" Timberline said into my ear.

"It isn't the girl," I said. "Next to her—that's the Archfiend."

Timberline studied Warren for a moment, then turned to me and I thought she was going to say something but she only smiled.

The drum stopped. The woman held the chicken up and with a short knife "killed" it—except I could see she didn't really kill it, though the chicken flapped its wings with great realism and then lay still in the old woman's hand, pretending to be a bundle of feathers. The chicken was apparently trained to "die" every show, and I thought how annoyed the voodoo gods must have felt. I also decided the time had come to have a word with Warren.

Mechanically I got up—scarcely murmuring an excuse to Timberline—and started across the room between the front tables and the stage. The act was over and the performers were retiring through a little curtained door at the rear of the stage. When I was halfway, I saw that Warren was slowly shaking his head and realized that he was signaling me to stay away. When he saw that I wasn't turning back, he quickly whispered something to Shill, got up, mounted the stage and disappeared through the curtained door. I hesitated again, ready to jump on

77

the stage and follow him, when I saw Gus standing in the penumbra of the stage lights looking at me in a way that said I was out of order. I had the impression he had caught a signal from Cy, or possibly from Warren; he shook his head once, in the negative. I continued across the room in front of the stage, my idea being to talk to Shill and wait for Warren to come back.

"Shill," I said when I got to her table, "I have to see him. What did he run off like that for?"

Her next line I had heard before, exactly the way she said it. It was from *The Big Sleep*, the nymphomaniac sister who falls into Bogart's arms. There was even a slight resemblance.

"You're cute."

"You're a lovely girl, Shill, but I have to see Warren this time. It's awfully important."

"Is it?"

"Yes. Very." She tossed her blonde hair like a fighter clearing his vision and her glance picked up Timberline in the process. Then she smiled politely, as she had probably been taught.

"My!"

"Look, it's—"

"—a matter of something and something?"

"That's right."

"But you haven't been playing the rules; you were supposed to come alone, remember?"

"What difference does that make? And look here—"

"Lots," she said, looking across at Timberline again, then back at me. I glanced at the drink she held in front of her. It looked like the bottom of a dirty aquarium. "Avery?"

"What?"

"Are you a frog?"

Suddenly I was exasperated. I wanted peace. I wanted Timberline. I wanted Warren to stop his theatrics.

"A Frog!" I shouted quite loudly. "You mean am I *French?* What kind of a stupid question is that?" (And only that afternoon, Timberline had asked me if I was English! "I am an *American!*" I remember thinking, but at the time found small comfort in the fact.) Out of the corner of my eye I spotted Gus-goon stomaching it among the tables, my way. Shill was smiling, enjoying my distress—but at the same time with a little searching "Help me please" look in her eyes which at the time I took for mockery. Beware, I told myself, of girls who are young and beautiful and ask fey riddles.

"Not French, silly," she said, tossing her hair aside again. It fell back. "Not *French*. A frog. Are you *the* Frog?"

A sudden smell of barbershop told me Gus was right behind me. I half-turned; he was. He started to say something disagreeable but Shill stopped him cold with a look.

"I'm a fox," she said to me, "and I can prove it to you." She laughed. I will admit my face must have appeared rather comical then. She laughed quite hard and then suddenly stopped laughing and, with a glance at Gus, leaned across the table to me. "I went to Foxcroft," she said solemnly, almost reverently, but with a note of challenge. "Have you ever heard of Foxcroft?"

Now Gus was gesturing with his head muscles that I should retire by the shortest route to my table.

"Yes," I said to Shill, then added wildly, "and I've also heard of fox-HUNTS!" I'm still not certain what I intended to mean—perhaps some childish counterthreat. She smiled.

"Not good, Avery," she said. "Almost good but that's the worst. You're trying, that's the trouble. You're trying to make sense out of everything but it's all the wrong kind of sense. Relax. Breathe deeply—it's good for you. Don't fight things so much. And don't forget about tomorrow night. Everything will be better for you. Very soon. Gus, this man is bothering me."

Fifteen minutes later, Timberline and I stood together under the great fluted phallus of Coit Tower on Telegraph Hill watching a freighter's lights slide toward the Golden Gate Bridge. The air was cool and fragrant with eucalyptus, the sky was full of stars, Timberline was furious. I had already tried to apologize for my leaving our table at the Hawk Club. I tried again.

"I am sorry about leaving you that way. I had to see those people. A question of—"

"I know, your aunt. You don't have to explain anything."

"Well, it's just possible that man you saw with the dark circles around his eyes is really trying to kill her."

"Maybe you ought to call the police," suggested Timberline icily.

"But he hasn't done anything yet. And besides, the worst of it is—I mean, if you look at it a certain way—I'm partly to blame."

"Then maybe you ought to call a psychiatrist," she advised. Out on the Bay a boat horn sounded. I didn't say anything.

"Why do you think you're to blame?" she asked, still coldly but with her temper now slightly thawed by curiosity.

"You wouldn't believe it anyway," I said.

"Who was that girl, for instance? The one with no expression on her face."

"She went to Foxcroft," I explained. "Apparently now she's the Archfiend's girl friend."

"And that Patricia. I'll bet she went to a good school too?"

"Miss Burke's. Oh, Patricia's all right, once you—"

"It's too bad."

"What is?"

"We're really class enemies."

"But I haven't got a bean!" I protested. "Besides, how can you just—lump people together like that?"

"But you do have expectations?" she persisted in an accusing tone.

"Very remote ones," I said tentatively. "I never think about them."

We watched the freighter's lights disappear past the bridge tower.

"Tell me about your parents," I said. "Your father, for instance."

"He isn't my real father. St. Denis is my mother's name. We live on top of a warehouse in New York. I told you that."

I said I didn't know people could live on warehouses in New York and she explained that it was on account of a special lease—the owner couldn't force them out.

"It's a whole loft, a big place like a penthouse almost, but not really. It isn't the least bit luxurious. I have a huge studio." She looked at me, frowning, as if she was doubtful if I could understand what she was saying. "It's a terrific mess always. My father makes mannequin molds. At home. And he leaves teacups around on the floor and on the piano. My father leaves teacups *everywhere*. It's terrifically disorderly."

"Sounds marvelous," I said. Somehow, it did.

"We used to have a maid who came in."

"Not any more?"

"She stopped coming on account of the elevator man."

"He's awful?"

"Horrible."

Together we looked out at the electronic beauty of the city. A breeze stirred the eucalyptus leaves over our heads and I felt her hand tuck under my arm.

A few minutes later, I walked her down the wooden stairs to her friend's house. Her friend was inside and we kissed good night at the door.

82

THE

CONTRACT

---

769. COMPACT.—*N.* compact, contract, agreement, bargain; affidation; pact, -ion; bond, covenant, indenture.

stipulation, settlement, convention; compromise, *cartel.*

protocol, treaty, *concordat, Zollverein, Sonderbund,* charter, *Magna Charta,* Pragmatic Sanction.

make –, strike- a bargain; come to -terms, – an understanding; compromise &c. 774; set at rest; close, – with; conclude, complete, settle; confirm, ratify, clench, subscribe, underwrite; en-, in-dorse; put the seal to; sign, seal &c. (*attest*) 467; indent.

take one at one's word, bargain by inch of candle.

Adj. agreed &c. *v.*; conventional; under hand and seal.

Phr. caveat emptor.

WARREN'S Aunt June lives in an historic old firetrap on Franklin Street which I have always thought of as the perfect house if you happen to be a bat. Architecturally it is a patchwork of "General Grant," Byzantine, Gothic and Arabic styles, with certain knobby elements which are probably uniquely San Franciscan. Pigeons shuffle around its minarets and gables and roost under the eaves and sun themselves on the TV antenna. The whole house is painted mocha. Aunt June, who could afford to live anywhere, lives here; in fact, she seldom leaves the house and is considered by San Francisco to be "strange." Ask Shag.

At nine sharp that next evening, he and I creaked up the long flight of stairs from the street and pulled the bell. There was a small Cambodian festival inside, then silence. A full minute later, a little panel in the door snapped open revealing Warren's horn-rimmed eyes. The peekhole closed, a chain fell, a bolt slid, the latch clicked and there was Warren, wearing an old-fashioned smoking jacket, looking at his watch.

"Excellent," he said.

We entered a large dim hall, at the farther end of which an opaline haze shifted ectoplasmically. Three rapid gunshots rang out, followed by an endless squealing of car brakes, silence, then a sickening crash and an explosion. Warren listened with his head cocked like a piano tuner.

"That's only the telly," he explained. "Auntie June's favorite hour of violence and—what's the word?—mayhem." He motioned us toward a parlor on the right, adding, "So we don't have anything to worry about for—fifty minutes. She's in another world."

It was a large room in which it was impossible to advance three feet in a straight line in any direction. The light from varous Tiffany and fringe-shaped lamps revealed a veritable Matto Grosso of bric-a-brac and quirkish furnishings, among which I noted a cut-glass bowl offering petrified nuts, clocks sous verre, an aspidistra, Dresden birds, stuffed birds, an apparently living myna bird, a small replica of the Laocoön, a wicker saddle, an Oriental gong. The walls were almost completely covered with pictures, notably a great somber oil of no identifiable subject ("Yosemite Dawn," the legend on the gold frame claimed), flower prints, still lifes, gladiatorial contests, and grizzly bears. Shag and I followed Warren through this jungle to a small clearing.

"I've never really cared for this room," said Warren as we sat down cautiously in protesting antiques; "too—what shall we call it?—Victorian for my taste. My uncle hated it, but then my uncle hated everything, beginning with himself. How are you both managing?"

"Fine," I said.

"Can't complain," said Shag. "How's yourself?"

"Oh, I keep busy," said Warren. "Of course, nothing is so enviable as looking after our dear aunts' little portfolios. So they really pay you a salary for that sort of work, Shag?" Shag laughed unconvincingly and Warren turned to me.

"Incidentally, Avery, sorry about last night but I didn't think it was—prudent for that girl to see us—consorting together. No, that's wrong, isn't it? Simply 'consorting' would be more correct, wouldn't it? She was very attractive but I didn't know who she was, you see. No sense in taking chances where the Contract's concerned, is there?"

"That's what we wanted to talk to you about," I said.

"Yeah," added the silver-tongued lawyer.

"And that's what we're here for," said Warren, looking at us with odd little Northern Lights in his eyes. "And Avery, wasn't it prophetic we should meet that way at the airport? I think it augurs rather well—"

"Warren," I said, "let's get one thing straight: you aren't really *serious* about that so-called Contract, are you?"

"Dead serious. Oh, yes. Dead serious." He looked pleased, as if he had expected the question. From across the hall we heard a series of grunts and crashes that sounded like a chase through a glass works.

"Well, this may come as a surprise to you," I said, "but Shag and I weren't."

"No," said Shag.

"What a pity."

"So," I went on, "for a thing like that to—work, we'd have to all take it as seriously as you do. Wouldn't we?"

"Not necessarily." Silence. Then: "We have a contract. Ask Shag. He'll tell you about the sanctity—I think that's the usual term—of contracts."

"Not illegal contracts," said Shag. "They aren't sanctified."

"Get out of here, June. Can't you see I'm busy?" Startled, Shag and I looked around for the voice. It was the myna bird. Warren explained that the bird had picked up several expressions from his late uncle, so that, while the former master of the house was gone, his foul disposition, so to speak, lingered on.

"Sometimes, Shag," Warren continued, "in my experience at least, you find that the more illegal an agreement, the more—binding. But I say nothing of this."

"You just did," I pointed out.

"O.K., Warren," Shag said, "but nobody would ever take a thing like that seriously. You can show it to anyone in San Francisco and they'd all see it was just a gag."

"Of course."

"Well?"

"If."

"Huh?"

"If."

"If what?" I asked.

Warren looked from one to the other of us, grinning in a way I didn't like.

"If one of its provisions isn't—already carried out."

88

The Contract

In the silence which followed, the bird said:
"I've got work to do! *Important* work to do!"

Shag and I glanced at each other. Warren looked suddenly distressed.

"But excuse my manners," he said. "I haven't even offered you drinks. No wonder we're—starting off on the wrong foot." He got up and went over to what looked like a rattan catafalque and opened the top. "What's your pleasure?"

"Elderberry wine," I said.

We settled for Scotch. Warren mixed the highballs with fanatical precision, using a jigger. When he came back with the drinks, he acted is if he'd forgotten what we had just been talking about.

"Servants' night out," he said, "and just as well, isn't it? There's only one anyway—the same Cecilia she's had for years. Poor Cecilia, she's getting almost as—what shall I say?—peculiar as Auntie June. Did I tell you that my sainted aunt has visions of joining me in my—nefarious existence? Yes. Instead of making an honest man of me by discreetly passing away, she has a senile fixation about wanting to belong to what she thinks of as the 'underworld.' Imagine. I put it down to the effect of television. But I do trust Cecilia will be comfortably provided for. Shag—what? Something, hmm?"

"Uh-huh," said Shag.

"But don't look so unhappy," said Warren. "Look at the bright side. No one's going to suspect anything if we each do our part. And keep in mind that for every one of us a very great deal of money is at stake, a very great deal—" A strange look came over his face and he choked up. Then, when he'd pulled himself together, he went on, "Shag, our bookkeeper, could give us an idea, hmm? Of course in these brackets, Uncle Sam flattens it out pretty much, but in the end, after the probates, I wouldn't say any one of us would come off with less than —what?—three million? Four? And that's enough to live pretty comfortably for a while in this—what does the poet call it?—'little life that's rounded by a sleep.' "

"But we're talking about murder!" I protested.

"That's the trouble," said Warren.

"Of course it's the trouble!"

"No, I mean you don't like the word."

"What word?"

"Murder. You don't like its associations."

"Associations! Good God, Warren! Murder is against the law. In this state it happens to be a capital crime. It is also very, very wrong!"

Warren smiled comfortably at us.

"Words," he stated. "Semantics."

Then, just as Shag and I were getting a clear message that Warren was sicker and a lot more dangerous than we had ever imagined, Warren proposed that we go downstairs. The Contract was downstairs. So we had to lockstep on tiptoes past the door of the darkened room where

The Contract

Aunt June was watching television (hearing, as we passed, only one soft whine of a video ricochet) and down steep cellar steps and through a laundry area to the gun room.

It had been his uncle's, Warren explained, and as fluorescent lights flickered on, we entered, up two stairs, a large concrete-floored room walled almost completely on either side wth hardwood-and-glass cases. There were several packing cases in the center of the room on the floor; one, I noticed marked

U S ARMY
THIS END UP

At the far end of the room I noticed an entrance to a dark area, which we were soon to learn was an indoor shooting range. In the glass cases were guns of every type, ancient and modern, pistols, rifles, shotguns, and even a sub-machine gun. In other cases there were crossbows, blowguns, krisses, spears, daggers, knives, swords, rapiers, in fact every utensil conceivable with which man has stabbed and perforated himself throughout the ages. It was a veritable Louvre of lethal weaponry.

But, of all this, the item Warren particularly drew our attention to was what he described as his own latest contribution to the collection; it lay in an open packing crate, a deadly-looking device with a stovepipe barrel and a box with knobs and an eyepiece at one end. He explained that we were looking at a Redeye rocket launcher of the latest type. Heat-seeking. With it, were

91

he so minded, one man could shoot down a low-flying jet. I asked Warren how he had happened to come by it, but he only grinned and said nothing.

Then we went over to a bench near the entrance to the shooting range, and from a drawer Warren took out the black attaché case I had seen him with at the airport. He unlocked it with a key from his pocket and still without a word took out a suddenly familiar-looking piece of ruled binder paper and spread it open on the bench. Shag and I approached. We read:

> WHEREAS the undersigned being of sound mind and body agree:
>
> *Article I:* that Avery Albright Ashley shall duly perform or effect the liquidation of one MRS. LORRILLARD PEABODY, a resident of the city and county of San Francisco.
>
> *Article II:* that Cedric "Shag" Bronston shall duly perform or effect the liquidation of one MRS. CRAIG OLIPHANT, a resident of the city and county of San Francisco.
>
> *Article III:* that Warren Thorp Oliphant II shall duly perform or effect the liquidation of one MRS. SEWARD VIGOREX, a resident of the city and county of San Francisco.
>
> WHEREAS it is further agreed that at least twenty-four (24) hours before the perform-

ance of each of said articles the Liquidator (sic.) shall give due notification to the Interested Signatory, to wit:

Article I   Cedric "Shag" Bronston
Article II   Warren Thorp Oliphant II
Article III   Avery Albright Ashley

THEREFORE, upon execution of this agreement in quail blood, it shall become a binding and irrevocable Contract between us.

(Signed)
Avery A. Ashley
Shag Bronston
Warren T. Oliphant II

Palm Springs,
California
June 10, 1955

"Bunny?"

The three of us froze. It was an elderly woman's voice. Warren's Aunt June.

"Are you in there?"

She was near the door now. Warren motioned to me and Shag to hide in the shooting range.

"Don't scare me now, Bunny. I know you're in there!" We heard her breathing heavily as she came up the stairs into the gun room.

"Scare you!" said Warren. "Auntie, I never scare you! What are you talking about?"

"I know it," she said. "Sometimes I wish you would— even 'boo' would be better than nothing."

"What brings you down here, Auntie?"

"Program's over."

From inside the shooting range, we couldn't see her but we could see Warren standing there with his hand resting on the Contract.

"What do you want, Auntie?"

"Me? Nothing. Ha! What would a rich old woman like me ever want? Ha! Ha!"

"Auntie, you better go up to bed. You're potted again."

"Don't talk smart!" she said, then instantly her voice became pleading. "Bunny, take me with you."

"We've been all through that," he told her. "The answer is no. For one thing, it wouldn't be safe for you down there."

"Fiddlesticks!" she said. "Besides, think anyone's safe up here with the Bat Burglar breaking into people's houses?" Then with an elaborate air of mystery, she sniffled and said, "Oh, I know."

"What do you know?"

94

"I know a nephew of mine who's just waiting around for me to be gone."

There was a long silence, then Warren said:

"Auntie, believe me, I'm not just waiting around for you to be gone."

She must have been down there about ten minutes before Warren got her started upstairs and headed off to "beddie." When we heard the floorboards creaking overhead, Shag and I came out of the shooting range, and a moment later Warren returned.

"Quite a character, isn't she?" he said to Shag. "Imagine a wealthy old woman like that wanting to embark on a career of crime. I find it immoral, don't you?"

Then he outlined his plan. As we listened, he paced back and forth in front of the gun cases like a briefing officer outlining an air strike, darting glances at Shag as he talked. At exactly 9:30 one week from that night, Shag would come to the house, enter by the basement door using a key Warren would give him, climb the stairs and proceed down the hallway to the sitting room, where the TV was. Aunt June would be there watching a program she never missed called GANGWAR. There would be plenty of shooting, and the one extra shot would never be noticed by the servant upstairs or anyone who happened to be passing the house. And in case anyone did see him entering or leaving, Shag would be wearing a bat mask like the Bat Burglar and he would steal some valuable on his way out to make it appear as a murder in the course of a robbery. Warren had it all figured out. As a matter of fact, he made it all sound fairly simple.

After a moment of reflection, Shag said he couldn't do it. Warren asked why not.

"I just couldn't, that's all," he said.

"Nonsense," said Warren, grinning his lemon grin. "Where there's a will, there's a way."

Shag said that was just the point—he didn't have the will—and then Warren pretended to be surprised and said, "Oh, but who said anything about *your* will?" Then, as if hurrying over an unpleasant minor point, he explained that he would be in Saint Sebastian when it happened and return again for the funeral and the settlement of the estate.

Shag asked why he should be the one to go first and Warren again pretended surprise:

"Oh, yes. Of course you'd be concerned about that. Even though the Contract's terms are perfectly clear and binding on all three of us. But don't worry—" He looked straight at me and, still talking to Shag, "—you won't be first!"

"He's crazy," was the first thing Shag said as we walked down the hill to his car.

"Apparently," I said. Between the time Warren had let us out the front door and that moment, an idea had been forming in my mind.

"What are we going to do, Ave?"

"Maybe you better just do what he says—"

Shag stopped dead and looked at me.

"—but not next Thursday. Say, on Monday. And not to kill Aunt June but to go back there and get the Contract. Once we have that, he can't blackmail us and we can have him put away in Agnew or Napa or some place."

We had reached Shag's Ford. We got in. He was thoughtful as he started the car.

"I can't Monday."

"Why not?"

"Chamber of Commerce meeting."

And so we settled on Tuesday instead of Monday.

A WARNING

668. WARNING.

handwriting on the wall, *tekel up-harsin,* yellow flag; fog-signal, -horn; monitor, warning voice, Cassandra, signs of the times, Mother Cary's chickens, stormy petrel, bird of ill omen, gathering clouds, clouds in the horizon, death-watch.

Adv. in terrorem &c. (*threat*) 909.

Int. beware! ware! take care! mind –, take care- what you are about! mind!

Phr. ne reveillez pas le chat qui dort; fœnum habet in cornu.

A totally insignificant figure in this narrative is Mr. Donahue, the night watchman privately engaged by some of the householders in Aunt Lavinia's neighborhood and ironically known as Old Flashlight. One seldom sees him and he is known to be fantastically unlucky about being anywhere when something is happening such as a housebreaking or a fire, but as he has been doing this work for a good many years everyone complains about him but no one seems willing to let him go. I mention Donahue only because when Shag dropped me off that night in front of Aunt Lavinia's house, he was out there in his Chevrolet across the street by the park, near the place I had seen Warren. At least Old Flashlight is on the job, I thought as I went inside.

And that night did, in fact, pass uneventfully.

The next morning it was raining. Aunt Lavinia was being driven down the Peninsula for lunch at the Burlingame Country Club. I spent most of the morning and part of the afternoon installing the new electric fuel pump in the Jag. In the course of the job, I found several new rust spots coming through the mouse-colored paint, the rubber around the stick shift was coming apart, and I realized I had lost rapport with the car. Once I had fancied the vehicle bespoke a certain je ne sais quoi (for a fact, girls had come skipping to pat the funny old thing and have a ride in it—"Oh, AVERY, it's JUST DIVINE!"), and in keeping with the informal atmosphere created by the sutures in the English leather, the baked woodwork, the fried safety glass, I kept the back seat and floor full of empty oil cans, spare parts, empty Kleenex boxes, Coke bottles, rags (and I think at least some of my fashionable young passengers welcomed a ride in Avery's Jag as sort of an escape from Mother)—but now I found it looked disgusting. I wondered how I could possibly continue to be seen driving such a wreck.

Then at five o'clock the phone rang. It was still raining. Aunt Lavinia was back, napping upstairs. I took the call in the library. It was Shill.

"I can't talk," she said. "That girl friend you were with at the club last night."

"What about her?"

"Just—she better be very careful tonight. He knows where she's staying."

That was all. She just said that and hung up.

Five minutes later, I was pounding on the door of Timberline's friend's house. There were still lights upstairs. The window opened and Timberline asked me what I was doing there.

"Let me in," I said. "It's important."

She hesitated a moment, then came down and opened the door for me. Just like that. By the light coming from upstairs, I saw that she was wearing a sort of mini-peignoir and was obviously ready for bed.

"Do you want a beer?" she asked me. I had expected her to be angry.

"Yes."

She went to the kitchen to get the beer and I watched her in the light from the refrigerator. "What's so important?" she said. "I thought you had to see a friend tonight."

I had told her that the night before—not that it was Warren, just that I had to see a friend.

"I did see him."

"The Archfiend?"

"Yes. How did you guess?"

"I guessed. Is he really trying to kill your aunt?" She opened the beer with a loud *psht* and brought it to me with a glass marked STRYCHNINE.

"It appears so," I said and took the beer and went to the window and looked up and down the street. There was no one there. "Has anyone phoned?"

"No," she said. "There isn't any phone."

"Is your friend upstairs?"

Timberline put a record on the turntable and set the arm on it. It was Mozart, I think.

"No," she said. "She's away till tomorrow night." She stretched out on the couch. "She said she was going to spend the night at a place called Piedmont. Have you ever heard of Piedmont?"

"Yes."

"Avery."

"What?"

"If your aunt's in danger, shouldn't you be doing something?"

I moved away from the window and came over and sat on the edge of the couch with my beer.

"Don't be alarmed," I said, "but you may be in danger, too."

"Who's alarmed?" she said.

The next morning, the first sounds I heard were the clanking of freight cars and a violent slap against a door, which was ajar. A folded *Chronicle* balanced on end for a moment, then half-turned and fell open on the floor. I read the headline:

SOCIALITE'S HOME BLASTED

"My God," I said.

"What's the matter?" said a girl's voice from another room. It was Timberline's. I remembered where I was.

"It was a TRAP!" I said, leaping off the couch to get the paper. Timberline came in from the kitchen. She was wearing blue jeans and a shirt and was carrying a coffee percolator and two brown ceramic cups. "My coming here was a TRAP!"

"Thanks," she said. "Coffee?"

I explained about Shill's warning as I dressed and tried

to read the paper at the same time. The article under the three-inch headline began:

> "At ten-thirty last night, a fiery explosion rocked the palatial Washington Street home of Mrs. Seward Vigorex, causing some damage. Mrs. Vigorex, widow of an international financier and prominent in San Francisco society, was at home at the time of the blast, but was not injured. Two servants also escaped injury. Police are investigating the possibility that the explosion was caused by a bomb intended for Mrs. Vigorex's neighbor, General—"

I thought with a certain relief: at least they haven't found out it was Warren!

"So you really did think I was in danger," said Timberline, reading the paper over my shoulder.

"Yes," I said, thinking: "Aunt Lavinia was really almost killed!"

Timberline suggested she go with me to Washington Street. I told her I didn't think my aunt would want to be seeing people just then. And I really believed that. It only shows how very little I knew about Aunt Lavinia and her circle.

POST-MORTEMS

AND

MRS. PEABODY

---

social -gathering, – *réunion;* assembly &c. (*assemblage*) 72; party, entertainment, reception, *levée,* at home, *conversazione, soirée, matinée;* evening –, morning –, afternoon –, gardenparty; kettle-, drum; *partie carrée,* dish of tea, *ridotto,* rout, house-warming; ball, festival &c. (*amusement*) 840; "the feast of reason and the flow of soul."

visit, -ing; round of visits; call, morning call.

THE park across the street from Aunt Lavinia's house is usually deserted on weekday mornings, but this morning it was full of people. Apparently everyone had read about the explosion and had come to the park to have a look at the house. There were nannies local and nannies extraterritorial, mothers with baby carriages, bachelors with dogs, a Japanese with a Nikon, and frayed spinsters from the genteel ghettos of California Street, up between music lessons. I had trouble parking. There were cars on both sides of the street for a block each way. In front of the house, I recognized the vintage LaSalle with the PRESS card which belongs to Connie Van Renseller Beasy; Connie herself was leaning on its fender feeding a sandwich to a policeman. Also, I spotted the Countess Byelakonskaya's black Volks and, as I might have suspected, Gordon Prescott-Peel's Barracuda convertible. I parked the Jag in Aunt Lavinia's service driveway down the hill, walked back up the street and around to the front gates so as not to frighten Cora-the-Cook (my own nerves were not ready just then for one of her Hitchcock screams), and went up to say hello to Connie.

"Come ON, Hammond," she was urging, "don't be a big baby. EAT it!" She saw me. "Avery!" she yelled. "Where have YOU been?" The policeman looked at me; it was the first time I could remember being intimidated by a guardian of the peace eating a cucumber sandwich from a girl reporter's hand.

"Hi, Connie," I parried. "What brings you here?"

"Are you kidding, Heart? Come ON, Hammond."

Now ordinarily I enjoy an astringent exchange with Connie Beasy, who at thirty-eight or -nine is San Francisco's star déclassée and a good scout: nice features and figure, bad complexion, eyes about as melting as bank doors, but always direct; in fact, sometimes you feel that Connie is in a trap of her own honesty, that, so to speak, her directness keeps her from enjoying ordinary casual relationships, though she tries. Two years of a doomed marriage to the first trumpet player of the Noble Sissle orchestra hasn't helped either, especially since the nuptials took place in Reno less than a year after her graduation from Miss Hamlin's School. Today her hair is combed from a side part in Gulf Streams of blonde in soft brown; that morning, she wore an oatmeal-colored suit with a short skirt, purchased no doubt in Paris but not by Connie, who gets her clothes from a second-floor Post Street boutique called Cast-offs, Inc. She is, as I say, a good scout, and you would hardly recognize her in the lush copy she turns out, with much ironical professional pride, for the *Chronicle*'s Society page. But Connie's cynicism does not run deep; one minute she will say something outrageous about the city's Establishment and the next she will take some mild remark of yours as a slur against the fairyland society of her dashed dreams and turn class-proud and Van Renseller, forgetting the dreams are dashed and that she never was the right Van Renseller in the first place.

Hammond ate the sandwich.

"You wive here, sir?" It took me a moment to decode him. I told him I did live here and who I was. Hammond listened, munching thoughtfully.

"Your aunt was wucky," he said solemnly, "weawee wucky."

As casually as I could, I asked if they knew who had thrown the bomb. Hammond looked at Connie. "Wait till Ham tells you his big news," she said.

"It wasn't no bomb, fehwa." He paused here for effect. I asked what it was.

"It was a WOCKET."

As I deciphered his message, I felt a sudden shock. The Redeye!

"A rocket!" I said. My reaction seemed to please Hammond.

"That's what I said—a weal miwitawee wocket."

"But—the radio said it was a bomb."

"Waydio says a wot of things, don't it?"

I felt suddenly weak and turned to Connie.

"See, Heart," she said, "your aunt's house and the Rodney place both look a little like the Taj Mahal, but imagine anyone making a boo-boo like firing a rocket into the wrong one."

"They wuh twying to get the genwal."

"No! I mean—that's what the inspector thinks happened?"

"That what the inspectah thinks, that's what the FBI thinks, that's what Ahmy Miwitawee Intewegence thinks, and that's what I think," said Hammond, adding, "Don't wowee, some of these guys get weawee dumb." It took me a second to realize that "these guys" meant the would-be assassins and not the forces of order. He asked Connie if she had any more sandwiches. Connie handed him the box; Hammond took two and started to leave.

"You mean," I said to him, "the FBI and Army Intelligence are investigating too?"

"You bet, fewah, that wocket was cwassified—bwand-new. The genwal's a powitical wefugee. Next time maybe them Weds won't miss!"

Weds! Good grief, they were blaming it on the Communists! As I watched Hammond returning to his post at the Rodney house, I almost felt like calling him back and explaining the Warren situation to him. Almost. Through the gates, I saw the front door of Aunt Lavinia's house standing open and unguarded. How, I wondered, could the inspector, the FBI, and Army Intelligence be so—unintelligent? But I didn't call him back. Though I realized that the stakes of our involvement with Warren had now been raised from conspiracy to complicity in an attempted murder, I told myself that this was not the time or the place for such a revelation. There would be time, I told myself, later.

"Don't tell me," I said to Connie, forcing frivolity into my voice, "that a little thing like a rocket going off in someone's house is a social event?"

"Depends whose house, Heart," said Connie. "In your aunt's case, a small firecracker would do the trick. Of course, I don't cover the news side; Bert got all he could last night from old Ferguson and the morgue. He was sort of interested in where you were, by the way. But me, all I'm interested in is the social angle—names and clothes."

"Here? This morning?"

"Society always knows where to be at a particular time, Heart; and this morning, it's here. Tonight it will be somewhere else, and they'll say, 'You know, darling, this morning I was over at Livvy Vigorex's and do you know she was absolutely marvelous.' Did you know, incidentally, that your aunt has been absolutely marvelous? Ask Witter. Witter is in there playing Poohbah, which is why I'm out here in the street. No, honey, frankly I prefer it; my copy comes out cleaner when I get things at a little remove, and right now the atmosphere in there is straight Shalimar. I don't see how a guy like you puts up with it. Me, I don't mind; at worst, I can say it's my job—and I get a kick out of it anyway, seeing it's my life. The hell with it. Oh, yes, I expect we'll do a nice little boxed feature, maybe on the front page with the news story: 'This morning, a few close friends gathered at the Washington Street home of Mrs. Seward Vigorex to inspect the rocket damage. Looking cool and collected in a lavender knit, the peripatetic "Livvy" Vigorex recently returned from a European junket with her handsome nephew, Avery Ashley, received her many callers in the library . . .' Et cetera."

"No," I said.

". . . 'Among the "regulars" were the Princess Byelakonskaya, wearing a size-20 beige Chanel and half the Imperial loot; Mrs. Everett Bush, known to her intimate friends as Lame Brain; Mrs. Reginald Pringle, deaf as ever; and representing the Younger Contingent, Mr. Gordon Prescott-Peel, livening up the festivities by pouring martinis from his own shaker bearing the Prescott-Peel crest; and the perennially popular post-post-post-deb . . .' " Connie stopped short and bit her lip.

"Pat?"

"Cerise wool number, saw it at Magnin's myself. Cute but a trifle safe, for me anyway—even if I could afford it, which I can't. So why be safe? By the way," she added, "what's all this I hear about you deserting the fashionable and well-fixed Miss B. for some Mystery Girl?"

"Wherever did you hear a thing like that?"

"My sources are confidential, but my advice is if you want to keep your affairs a dark secret don't go to El Matador with a beautiful sculptress from New York named Timberline St. Denis who's got a show opening at Freddie's. The lucky girl. Here I thought all the time the Mystery Girl would be Constance Van Renslipper, Everybody's Cinderella Girl. Here I keep seeing us off somewhere in some romantic place doing something marvelous for two—dancing in the rain or something."

"Sidewalk café."

"Genial proprietor. Understands."

"Organ grinder with a monk."

"Lewd little urchin hanging around. You slip him a quarter or a lira or something to get lost. Then the rain stops."

Suddenly, to my surprise, Connie dove into her purse for a handkerchief and blew her nose. In a moment, though, she was all reporter again; she put back the handkerchief, took out her notebook and asked me why my aunt kept a crocodile in the house. Just then, Witter appeared at the front door and squinted officiously at the sun.

"AVERY!" he called, when he caught sight of me through the gates. "AVERY, THANK GOD!"

"Alligator," I corrected Connie, watching Witter. "I don't know really; I think it must remind her of my uncle." Connie, also ignoring Witter, who was industriously approaching us, looked at me oddly.

"No," I said, "not that way. Clarence just reminds her of when he used to be around—sort of an association."

Witter had come through the gates and we both said hello to him as if we hadn't noticed him before. Witter, in turn, acted as if Connie was not present.

"Avery," he said, "do you realize we have been telephoning for you everywhere?"

"Well, here I am, Witter. How is Aunt Lavinia?"

"Your aunt," said Witter, "has been absolutely marvelous!" Connie threw me a wink, then said to Witter with mild impatience:

"Oh, Witter, for God's sake, don't be such an old hot dog."

Witter glared at Connie as if gauging the disparity between the offense and the offender's importance, then said icily:

"Mrs. Beasy, if you had the least consideration for other people, you wouldn't park that—*car* directly in front of this house where everyone has to climb over it. Come on, Avery."

But at that minute, a long black Armstrong-Sidley silently drew up on the other side of Connie's LaSalle, a uniformed driver got out to open the back door, and we saw the flash of blue feathers through the closed windows.

"Good Lord," said Witter.

"Isn't that Mrs. Peabody?" asked Connie. Witter nodded, apparently too moved to speak. Then I saw that Shag was with her, half-hidden behind her in the back seat. He popped forward. Connie made a note in her notebook.

"That's the nephew," said Witter.

"Of course, Avery's friend. What's his real first name, Avery? It isn't Shag, is it?"

"No, it's Cedric," I said. "C—e—d—r—i—c."

"I know how to spell Cedric," Connie told me. "I even know how to spell Ulric. I had a friend named Ulric once. What a bastard."

"Ssh," said Witter gently.

Now the driver opened the door and the massive, august figure of Mrs. Lorrillard Peabody appeared, supported by the driver and a stainless steel cane.

Post-Mortems and Mrs. Peabody

Connie, impressed now herself, asked in a low voice what color we would call Mrs. Peabody's hat.

After a moment's thought, Witter said cerulean.

At this point in Mrs. Peabody's emigration from the automobile I decided to go inside the house ahead of her. Among other considerations, it seemed better to me if Shag and I didn't arrive together. I said good-bye to Connie, who paid no attention to me, being totally absorbed by the pageant she was witnessing. However, my decision left Witter wondering whether to follow me and "produce" the errant nephew to Aunt Lavinia and the others inside or to stay and "produce" Mrs. Peabody. I think the presence of the uniformed driver and Shag decided him, and perhaps the hope of having time to produce both of us, and he quickly followed me through the gates calculating that in the next moment Mrs. Peabody would be blinded by the sun.

The library where Aunt Lavinia and her guests were gathered had once been Uncle Seward's preserve, where he would often work in the daytime and in the evening after dinner bring male guests to drink brandy and growl golf scores at each other. The books in the shelves are volumes of history, biographies of notable men, rare folios, tall books on architecture, landscape gardening, painting, fat volumes on exploration, mineral deposits, finance, the complete works of Conrad (the only fictional work in the collection), and a complete Theodore Roosevelt, bound in leather, the first volume vigorously signed "For Woodie, ever, Teddie." There is one locked glass case containing Uncle Seward's unique library of books on ballooning.

Aunt Lavinia was sitting in an armchair almost directly under the chandelier (a gift to my uncle from the King of Belgium), looking at me as I entered the room with an expression exactly midway between nobility and vacancy. On her right, wearing many rings and bracelets and a decidedly Pre-Revolutionary stare, was her friend the Princess Byelakonskaya; then, Gordon Prescott-Peel, wearing a hound's-tooth tweed jacket and yellow ascot, raising his martini to me in a mock salute, his foppish eyes avid, as usual, for goffs and scandal; Mrs. Reginald Pringle, nodding and smiling; Mrs. Everett Bush, turning to look at me as I entered with Witter; and between Mrs. Bush and Aunt Lavinia, Patricia, looking at me with an expression of mild irony.

"Avery," said my aunt.

"The Prodigal Nephew returned," said Gordon.

"It's Avery," said Mrs. Pringle.

"We've been wondering where you were," said Mrs. Bush.

"We certainly have," said Patricia.

I went over to Aunt Lavinia, kissed her powdered cheek and asked how she was feeling. François entered the room with a silver tray of small sandwiches. The phone on the desk rang.

"Well, I'm all right, Avery, but you've heard about the terrible explosion in the living room last night. Have you seen it? I've already called Freddie to have him see about doing it over. But where were you? Yes, Gordon, please answer it and let François pass the sandwiches. Yes—where were you last night? We've been calling everywhere. Witter has been absolutely marvelous. He even thought of calling out for sandwiches because he knew they'd be busy in the kitchen. Cora's been having a fit and may really be ill. But why didn't you call, Avery? What are they, François—tongue? But I'm not sure everyone likes tongue. Whatever made them think of sending tongue? I'm glad you do, Louise, but I'm not sure everyone— Cucumber? And cheese? Oh, well, then we're all right, aren't we. François, you know, really saved my life. Oh, yes. You see, I had come into the living room after dinner and sat down in my chair and picked up my crossword puzzle when François came in to remind me that Clarence had not been fed. I don't know how I could have forgotten after all these years; I must have been worrying about where you were, Avery. You see," she said, turning to Mrs. Bush, "I have given orders that when I am at home, no one else is to feed Clarence. I do it myself. We have a special refrigerator for the fish. Seward always used to feed Clarence himself and somehow—"

"Of course," said the Princess, who has a very bass voice. "We know all about it."

Still standing in the doorway, Witter, who had been casting increasingly anxious glances into the hall, now took advantage of the Princess' interruption to announce the arrival of Mrs. Peabody.

"Christine? How nice," said my aunt, her face clouding. "But will she be able to stand the stairs? I've often thought of having them—flattened somehow. I think that could be done, don't you, Avery? What is it, Gordon? Is it someone I ought to talk to? The Reverend Appleby? Of course, I'll talk to him. Witter, go and see if Christine is all right; tell her I'm talking on the telephone. Hello, William."

There was some confusion. Witter went out of the room. Aunt Lavinia listened to the voice on the phone (which from the chair I had taken, between Aunt Lavinia and Patricia, I heard as a faint ecclesiastical scratch), then from the hall we heard Mrs. Peabody: "No, no, get away from me, Witter! I can manage perfectly well. Perfectly!"

"To me," remarked the Princess, "there is nothing unusual about bombs. I have been bombed many times. In Petersburg, at time of Revolution, the Bolsheviks—"

But just then, as Aunt Lavinia hung up the phone, Witter was backing slowly into the room. From the hall came Mrs. Peabody's clear, measured voice:

"Now stop fussing, Witter. I am simply going to sit on this bench and rest a moment before I come in. I always do. Stay where you are, Lavinia."

I suppose that among San Francisco dowagers, Mrs. Lorrillard Peabody stands first, both on the score of seniority and of wealth (Shag, I have noticed, lowers his voice when he speaks of her portfolio); and in her sixty-odd years as a social leader in the city, it is universally agreed that she has performed an extraordinary amount

of secret good. Nowadays, she has retired to an apartment on top of Nob Hill, lending her large estate in
Hillsborough, south of San Francisco, to Shag's widowed
mother and Mrs. Peabody's own first cousin George Van
Timkin and his wife Esther, in turn. She seldom attends
Opera openings, the Symphony, or the theater, but you
can sometimes see her on a good Sunday walking on her
driver's arm across the little park at Nob Hill to Grace
Cathedral; or perhaps you will see her in her Armstrong-
Sidley going up and down the hills of San Francisco on
purposeful rounds of mercy and improvement. The
flower sellers all recognize her and cable-car gripmen
ring their bells to her.

For as long as I can remember, Aunt Lavinia has taken
the position that Mrs. Peabody's survival is one of the
gerontological wonders of San Francisco, while Mrs. Peabody, in turn, has always treated Aunt Lavinia as if her
continued existence on earth was a tribute to my aunt's
"spirit" as well as to medical science. As for Shag, he
has never been on easy terms with his aunt, partly, I
suppose, because Bronson is basically a materialist, a practical man, and definitely dollar-oriented, while Mrs. Peabody prizes only such qualities as independence, "spirit"
(one of her favorite words), "quality," and "character,"
regarding her own millions as being of no importance,
except insofar as they confer upon her a dreadful responsibility. I have always liked Mrs. Peabody, and we have
shared an understanding based originally on a common
appreciation of ginger cookies and backgammon; but as
she appeared in the library doorway, supported by Shag,

her driver, and her steel cane, I suddenly found myself wondering whether she might not be the one to see through, somehow, to the secret of the Contract. Shag looked at me with such an expression of distress that I wished, just then, that my "accomplice" was a more subtle fellow.

"My dear," said Mrs. Peabody to Aunt Lavinia, who rose to greet her, "I came the moment I read it in the newspapers this morning. I flew. How are you?"

"Perfectly fine, Christine," said my aunt. "It takes more than a rocket to disturb me, you know. Everyone's making such a fuss over me. I have no idea why. I'm delighted you should think of coming, though of course it's very wicked and foolish of you."

She and Mrs. Peabody kissed, like French generals.

Then, saying good morning to me and finally to everyone at large, Mrs. Peabody, tended by Aunt Lavinia on one side, the driver on the other, slowly approached a chair I drew back for her and settled into it, dismissed her driver and, as Aunt Lavinia returned to her place and we men resumed our seats, began taking off her gloves.

"Don't pay the slightest attention to me," she said. "I want to hear everything. Go on just as you were. Avery, why on earth are you wearing smoked glasses in the house?" I had forgotten I was. I took them off. "That's much better—now I can see you. How are you?"

"Fine, Mrs. Peabody."

"Good. Playing backgammon?"

"No."

Aunt Lavinia's smile looked like the end of a glacier in a warm spring. "We were just talking about my explosion, Christine," she said.

"I want to hear every word."

And so as Mrs. Peabody listened with a look of intense absorption, pulling systematically on the fingers of her gloves, Aunt Lavinia reviewed her account of François' timely interruption and her leaving the living room to feed Clarence.

". . . so you see, when François met me with the bucket of fish, it must have been about half-past eight. I remember noticing how clean the tank was and then I remembered it was Mr. Spilker's day; we have a man from Fleishacker Zoo who comes every two weeks to clean the tank and look after Clarence and yesterday was his day. I had just begun feeding Clarence when I heard this really UNEARTHLY noise over my head; the whole house seemed to be shaking and I saw the glow of flames in the Conservatory window, and I thought of the Fire—"

"Well, of COURSE you did!" said Mrs. Peabody with approval, having now completely recovered herself. "Those of us who went through it will never forget it, never!" She addressed the Princess across the circle. "It wasn't so much the physical danger, you see, or the dreadful loss, everything going up in flame—you remember the spirit; I shall never forget the spirit it brought out in people—all SORTS of people in whom you'd never expect it. Social distinctions were absolutely abolished during the whole emergency. Everyone pitched in. Share and share alike. That's San Francisco at bottom, you know. Didn't matter what you HAD— you'd probably lost everything anyway—it was what you WERE that mattered, the rest was all meaningless, meaningless! It was what you really WERE—" With one glove half off, Mrs. Peabody was with her other hand clutching at the air in front of her face, as if she was trying physically to seize her recollection.

"What fire it was?" asked the Princess, to everyone's consternation. Mrs. Peabody, who was caught by surprise at a moment when her emotions were tightly wound up, made such a sudden effort to reply to the Princess that she began to cough and managed to retain control of the conversation only by pounding her steel cane loudly and rapidly on the carpet.

"THE Fire," she said when she had recovered sufficiently, "is what we call the San Francisco Earthquake and Fire of nineteen hundred and six. We call it the Fire inasmuch as it was the fire that did the real damage. It was, course, without any question, the greatest single disaster in this century. Anywhere."

"Pardon me, madame," said the Princess, "I think you forget Russian Revolution."

"Not at all," said Mrs. Peabody, without hesitation. "I'm speaking of spirit. You won't find the same sort of spirit in the Russian Revolution, no indeed—everyone forgetting class distinctions as if they never existed, everyone—" As Mrs. Peabody began shaking her fist,

Post-Mortems and Mrs. Peabody

François stepped forward with a tray of sandwiches; Mrs. Peabody looked at them and declared firmly that she wasn't going to eat anything.

"I felt the same spirit today," said Aunt Lavinia, taking advantage of her friend's momentary distraction. "Everyone has been absolutely marvelous. Who have I seen, Witter? The police, the FBI, the reporters, that nice man from the Army, my insurance man—they're taking care of everything, you know; and Shag's firm, my estate people, thought to have Podesta's send over a lovely pot of stephanosis. And, Avery, the inspector called to say he would be coming again." (Why, I wondered, had she directed this information at me? Was the chemistry of my ambiguous relationship with the inspector obvious even to Aunt Lavinia?) "And, oh yes, just as you were arriving, Christine, William called with a thought for me. He said the first thing he thought of when he saw the report on television was the Twenty-third Psalm—"

"I wish—William would—marry again," said Mrs. Pringle, expressing a thought that was universally shared by the widows and out of circulation as a topic of conversation for several years; only Mrs. Bush bothered to nod an acknowledgment to the speaker.

"You know, of course, they all told me not to come," resumed Mrs. Peabody. "My doctor said absolutely not. But then, all the dear man ever says is absolutely not. You know him, my dear? Proctor? Such an unfortunate name for a physician anyway—Doctor Proctor. Well, of course, he can't help that. And people tell me he's the most brilliant doctor in the city, and I haven't the slightest reason to doubt it. However, I'm quite sure that had I listened to all his fussing and precautions over the years, I shouldn't be here now. I don't quite have it in me to tell him I've attended the funerals of four of his predecessors who told me to slow down. Yes. But here we are talking about doctors and the Russian Revolution and I don't know what and you've had this terrible experience, Lavinia. Do you want to talk about it yet? Well, of course you do. No good bottling it up. I wouldn't myself. What I admire is the way you've managed to keep such control—you've kept control—" She had one glove completely off now and was starting on the other and suddenly began shaking her purplish hand violently as if in an effort to shake her meaning free.

"Lavinia has been splendid," said Witter, as though to help Mrs. Peabody through her little difficulty, but Mrs. Peabody being aware of no difficulty looked sharply at him.

"Where were you when the thing went off, Witter?"

"In my own flat," he said, closing his eyes, "fixing myself a little supper."

"I remember Society before the Fire," she resumed again, now on another tack; "it's not at all the same now. People seem to have lost all sense of value. I used to watch a great deal of television; I don't any more. Stopped the day Bennett Cerf went off the air. I don't happen to enjoy watching violence or war, we've had enough of that. And I won't watch comedy for the very good reason it isn't funny. I believe comedy should be funny, so I don't watch any of it. I read a great deal now."

Here Mrs. Peabody was overtaken by another coughing fit and a general conversation followed on the subject of murder mysteries. All the widows were avid readers of them, and they all had their favorite authors: Agatha Christie, Mary Roberts Rinehart, Raymond Chandler, Rex Stout. I re-lit my pipe and settled back in an attitude of judicious interest, suddenly wondering: How far would Warren go? What would I do if he kept on with his mad plan?

"Of course," said Mrs. Peabody, having recovered again, "in the end, there's nothing like the real thing. I knew old Harry Oakes, poor fellow. There's a mystery for you—never really solved, you know, though I have my own opinions. Money attracts murder like a flower attracts a bee. I have no idea why. Money is responsibility, nothing else." (Here Witter closed his eyes and nodded fervent agreement.) "If people only knew what it was, they wouldn't envy those of us who have it as they do. I blame it on the press, the sensationalism, the emphasis. I met old Mr. Hearst once and I told him I had a bone to pick with him and then I told him exactly what I'm telling you. And do you know what he told me? He agreed with me! He said the public has a voracious curiosity about everything that doesn't concern it and particularly about people who happen to have something. He said furthermore that the public dictated what went into his papers! Imagine it! William

Randolph Hearst admitted to me that the *people* dictated what went into his paper! I've been burglarized eight separate times and once my eye was blacked. And, naturally, every time it's been in the papers and every time someone else picks up the newspaper and says, 'Oh, what a simply lovely idea. I'll just go over and rob old Mrs. Peabody.' And they *do*. I know exactly how they get in, too: the night man in my apartment building sleeps exactly like the Fat Boy in Dickens. I read a great deal of Dickens now. Yes, they walk right by my Fat Boy—one of them had even been to Yale." Mrs. Peabody frowned, as if some distressing thought she chose not to repeat had crossed her mind, then looked fixedly at my aunt. "I don't want to alarm you, Lavinia, but I should be most careful, if I were you, until the police are certain who fired that thing into your living room last night."

"Oh, but Christine," my aunt replied, "the inspector was quite sure it was intended for the general next door. So was the young man from the FBI and that pleasant officer. It was the Communists, they think. Nothing was taken here, you see, and who would want to have me simply done away with if it wasn't to take something?"

"And there were those telephone threats," I said, wondering why I was speaking. Everyone in the room looked at me.

Aunt Lavinia
Mrs. Peabody
Patricia
Witter
Mrs. Bush

Post-Mortems and Mrs. Peabody

Gordon
Mrs. Pringle
the Princess
Shag
Then there were three more people, standing in the entrance from the hall.

the inspector
Freddie Van Deusen
Timberline
It took me a moment to realize that Timberline must have gone to Freddie's gallery after I left her, met Freddie there, learned that Aunt Lavinia had called for him, and simply come along. The inspector was watching me with a horrible *coy* look as I pieced this theory together. The attention of everyone seated in the room, however, was at once diverted from me to the newcomers. Freddie stepped forward with a huge box of yellow roses bedded in forest-green tissue.

"The Greeks—bearing gifts!" he announced, advancing into the room with the flower box. He made a point of noticing no one but Aunt Lavinia. "I asked myself what would be *right* for an explosion and I decided on yellow roses."

"Very thoughtful, Freddie," said Aunt Lavinia, rising. "Have François put them in water, Avery. Hello, Inspector." Witter was examining the roses for possible imperfections as I took them from Freddie. Timberline, in a simple beige dress, stood in the doorway looking at the ceilings, the people, the books on the shelves, as if she were a visitor from another planet. Holding the roses,

I looked at her, but when our eyes met, I felt she was not seeing me at all but just another figure in Aunt Lavinia's Washington Street waxworks.

At the same time, I felt Patricia's fingers at my throat, straightening my tie.

Freddie presented Timberline to Aunt Lavinia, who presented her and the inspector to the others in the room, and it was found that while Mrs. Peabody was acquainted with the inspector, who had investigated her robberies, she had never met Freddie.

"I'm merely a newcomer to San Francisco," he said. "A rank newcomer. That's why."

I noticed with satisfaction that Mrs. Peabody was not taken in by Freddie.

"Well, of course you are, young man," she said, "and I expect you are quite busy making an advantage of it. All's fair, but don't go trying to fool an old bird like me. My grandmother took in miners' washing, you know."

Freddie received this salvo with a frozen smile, then, after a second's calculation, turned to Aunt Lavinia and said that all the most interesting things always happened to Livvy Vigorex.

"Oh, not really, Freddie," protested my aunt, very pleased. "After all, the explosion here was an accident. I can't take the credit for it. Can I, Inspector?"

Ferguson looked at me and fingered his hat. Out of the corner of my eye, I noticed Shag staring at us. Kee-kee came in, sniffed the inspector's leg, then, unimpressed, went over and jumped into Aunt Lavinia's lap and started blinking at everyone.

Post-Mortems and Mrs. Peabody

"That's right, Mrs. Vigorex," he said. "That is—that's what we think." (Another "significant" glance at me.)

"Come over here, my dear," interrupted Mrs. Peabody, addressing Timberline, who was still standing. "Sit down next to me in this chair. That is, if you don't mind sitting next to an old museum piece." Timberline obligingly went over and sat in the chair next to Mrs. Peabody. Then, as she found herself momentarily the center of attention, she smiled brilliantly at me and said, "Hello, Avery."

"Oh, you're acquainted," said Aunt Lavinia, puzzled; then, seeing I still held the roses, added, "Do take Freddie's flowers, Avery."

Feeling piqued with my aunt for treating me like a dependent in front of Timberline and the others, I went downstairs and directly down the hall and into the kitchen without the usual scratching at the door and cooing Cora's name to allay her fears. As I shoved through the swinging doors, Cora was planted in front of the stove fighting with something hot and steaming in the oven. She turned and saw me, screamed lustily, buried her face in her pot holders, allowing a great sizzling bird to glide slowly into view. With another outcry she shoved the pan back in and slammed the oven door. I tossed Freddie's roses casually on the kitchen table and told her curtly to have François put them in something, then went back upstairs feeling better.

As I came into the library Freddie was saying that he thought he'd heard the explosion. ("I was at Cindy Vendable's. It made a sort of boom.")

"I was in Burlingame," said Gordon, apparently hoping someone would ask him at whose house, but no one did.

"And what part of New York do you come from, my dear?" asked Mrs. Peabody, who had been conversing apart with Timberline while I'd been downstairs. "I used to go to New York a great deal but I don't now for the simple reason that all my old friends there are dead. Besides, it's such a nuisance getting me on and off the trains and I won't fly. I simply won't chew gum."

Timberline explained that she lived with her parents near Greenwich Village, adding—with a defiant glance at me and Patricia—that their apartment was over a warehouse.

"Oh!" said Mrs. Bush. "How—nice!"

"I told you she was original," said Freddie.

"My," said Mrs. Pringle.

Aunt Lavinia said, "I've never heard of anyone living over a warehouse, but then I can't think of any reason why one shouldn't." Witter and my aunt then looked at each other with identical expressions which were at once blank and full of significance.

Then Patricia said, "It must get cold."

Timberline's smile was sweet and deadly.

"Never where there are human beings," she said.

"N'est-pas!" cried Mrs. Peabody, very strongly moved. "N'est-pas! And of course I know the area," she went on triumphantly. "I used to visit old Mrs. Fish on Gramercy Park!" François came in with the roses in a crystal vase, set them carefully on the Regency desk behind Aunt Lavinia, and left.

Post-Mortems and Mrs. Peabody

"Well, now I think we know where Avery was last night," said Patricia, now looking deadly herself.

"Where?" asked Mrs. Bush. Everyone else was silent.

"He was with me," said Timberline, adding calmly, "—until about one."

"But you weren't home all night, Avery," said my aunt. "Where were you the other part of the night?"

I hesitated. Gordon was grinning at me as if he was already carving me up into stories to serve around town. I had to cover Timberline's lie—gallantry as well as prudence demanded it—but how? Just then, I happened to look at Shag—

"Come, dear boy," insisted Mrs. Peabody with a tap of her cane on the carpet, "it is necessary for you to tell the truth, or a version of the truth, or else a very good falsehood. People have a way of imagining the most extraordinary things when they're kept in the dark, you know."

I said I was at Shag's place the rest of the night.

"*Very* good," said Mrs. Peabody quickly with a sharp glance at Shag, who looked distressed.

"That's right. He was at my place," he managed to say—but I realized that something was rather wrong. Before I could guess what it was, Mrs. Peabody had turned to Timberline and said:

"My dear, I think I am going to call you Sunbird."

Inspector Ferguson and Aunt Lavinia led the way into the living room and the rest of us followed, Shag and I last, escorting Mrs. Peabody. Everyone gathered in the center of the huge room facing the damaged west end. The ceilings looked as if a Boy Scout troop had been building bonfires under them; one corner of the fireplace was demolished, there was shattered porcelain and crystal everywhere; the walls were pocked, curtains and upholstery tattered and burned; Aunt Lavinia's wing-back chair was kneeling forward on one stump of a leg; the French doors to the left of the fireplace were smashed, the frames shattered; over the mantelpiece, the portrait of Uncle Seward still hung on, but askew. Mrs. Peabody, the last to arrive in the room, was first to break the silence:

"Oh, Lavinia, your beautiful Sung vases, but what does it matter? The important thing is that you weren't injured. Oh, Inspector, can't something be done about these outrages?"

Ferguson replied that the police did its best and I waited for his sly glance in my direction, but it didn't come; now he had adopted a game of not looking at me at all. He began explaining (directing his remarks specifically at Mrs. Bush) how the rocket had entered the French doors leading to the balcony and struck the fireplace. He showed that the angle of entry and impact indicated that it was fired from the park. Freddie, meanwhile, had drawn Aunt Lavinia aside and was telling her his ideas for the remodeling. Mrs. Peabody, vibrating with emotion, put several more questions to the inspector.

Finally, everyone left the living room and was saying good-bye to my aunt in the hall, while Gordon ran around organizing a luncheon party at Señor Pico's, which was to include, I gathered, everyone except Mrs. Bush, Mrs. Pringle and the Princess. Mrs. Peabody was invited but declined, saying that her cook would never forgive her. Everyone moved slowly out into the sun-etched courtyard. Timberline came up to say good-bye to Mrs. Peabody, who took her hand. I realized then that the old lady was tiring fast.

"Well, my dear," she said, "I'm glad I came and partly on your account. The young people. You're from New York, you said. I travel less now, it's getting difficult to get me around and—" She let her driver, Henry, take my place at her side "—and, you see, I can't afford to let myself be—disappointed any more." She paused to consider the sense of her own words, then added: "But then, I never am, am I? Certainly not this lovely morning." Then, realizing that I had stepped away from her, she turned to me.

"Take care, Avery," she said, her gray eyes searching me coolly from the blue shadow of her aged face. "And if you ever want to have a talk, come and see me the way you used to do."

I didn't look at Shag.

"I will, Mrs. Peabody."

Then, as Gordon secretively marshaled the luncheon party, Mrs. Peabody went out through the gates and I followed. Connie Beasy was gone, no doubt back to her *Chronicle* cubbyhole to pound out the story of the matinee at Mrs. Vigorex's. Mrs. Peabody climbed in her car, and as the driver went around and got in, Shag threw me a desperate look and got in too. The Armstrong-

Sidley pulled away and I watched the pigtail of exhaust curling down the street. Then I happened to glance across to the park.

Gordon came up to me and whispered that I should go in Freddie's Mercedes. Gordon said he would take Aunt Lavinia and Patricia in his car as soon as Mrs. Rush and the Princess left (Mrs. Pringle had already gone). I told him to tell Freddie to go ahead, I said I would follow in my own car. I could almost hear Gordon's social computer whirring: he must have decided that I didn't want to go in Freddie's car with Timberline on account of Patricia. I let him believe what he wanted and watched him leave. But this wasn't the reason.

Across the street in the park, on the bench where the knitting nurses had been, Shill was waiting for me.

I had no intention of joining that merry lunch.

"Hello, Mr. Frog."

A kid's football rolled under her bench. She reached down for it and heaved it to a hot little guy wiping his nose on his sleeve. It was a girl's throw. Shill was definitely girl. She settled her ironic smile on me and eased back against the green slat park bench in a movement which somehow (I can't explain why) made the bench look like an illustration in a bench catalogue. As for Shill herself, she suddenly looked viciously attractive.

"You said Timberline was in danger. Timberline wasn't in danger," I told her.

She looked at me a very long time, then, without smiling any more, she said, "You don't know how it hurt me to tell you that; I had to. Sit down." She patted the bench beside her. I sat down.

"What about those rules?" I said.

"Rules were meant to be broken, weren't they?" Then she added in a hard but listless voice, "You're wanted."

"Warren wants me?"

"I said you're wanted, didn't I? What else could that mean?" She was looking at me as if she expected an answer. The midget football game was on top of us now. Kids were yelling numbers, hiking, skidding on the grass just behind our bench. I tried to concentrate on Aunt Lavinia's predicament.

"Well, I want to see him again, too," I parried, "and the quicker the better. This crazy thing has got to be stopped now." I was sure this last statement would bring back her ironic smile. It didn't.

"Maybe there's—another way."

"What's that?"

As I asked the question, I found the unexpected answer on Shill's half-parted lips. I stood up.

"Take me to Warren!" I ordered, suddenly thinking of Timberline.

I guess I will never know now exactly what happened that afternoon at the Hawk Club because the next two hours are still almost a total blank. I partly remember driving downtown with Shill in a blue Mustang she said Warren had rented; I even remember there was a minor traffic accident at the corner of Pacific and Leavenworth. Then, in the dark, empty club, I have a vague recollection of Warren arguing savagely with an old man with a mop and a bucket of Cloroxed water (I remember the smell of the Clorox), Warren telling the man to get out. And the lights—wildly throbbing lights . . .

I CALL ON

MRS. PEABODY

361. [Destruction of life; violent death.] KILLING.—*N.* killing &c. *v.*; homicide, manslaughter, murder, assassination, trucidation, occision; effusion of blood; blood, -shed; gore, slaughter, carnage, butchery.

massacre; *fusillade, noyade;* Thuggism.

death blow, finishing stroke, *coup de grâce, quietus.*

fatal accident, violent death, casualty.

V. kill, put to death, slay, shed blood; murder, assassinate, butcher, slaughter; victimize, immolate; massacre; take away -, deprive of- life; make away with, put an end to; despatch, dispatch; burke, settle, do for.

Tʜᴀᴛ night the fog laid a clammy hand on the city.

I stood near the iron fence of the Pacific Union Club, facing the heavy grilled glass doors of Mrs. Peabody's apartment on Sacramento Street. On my right, the cars under the great porte-cochère of the Fairmont Hotel made cubistic shadows in the swirling fog, a 1930s Pierce Arrow ad; the people coming in and out the revolving doors looked air-brushed. I listened to the Detroit-tuned door slams, drunken shouts, laughter, foghorns, and waited.

The doorman at the apartment house had left fifteen minutes earlier. The fat night man sat slumped over his stomach in the lobby, already nodding. Again, I counted up ten floors to the faintly lighted windows. I put my hands in the pockets of my trench coat, feeling the key and the gun . . .

"Who is it?"

In the semidark foyer, I said my name.

"Avery Ashley?" said Mrs. Peabody, as I came in the

living room. "Well, whatever are you doing here at this
hour? You gave me a start. You see, I didn't hear Mary
letting you in, thought she'd gone to bed long ago."

The vast, opulent living room was softly lit, a harmonious meeting of Western and Oriental styles, taste and
money. Mrs. Peabody herself sat in a persimmon-colored
armchair, holding a book in her lap, looking at me.

"Of course I'm always glad to see you," she went on.
"Wish you'd come more often, the way you used to.
Have an apple." She gestured with the back of her
guarded polychromatic hand to a silver bowl of fruit on
a table near where I stood. "Naturally, you young people
grow up, have no time for—Avery Ashley, why are you
pointing that gun at me?"

"I've—I've come to murder you, Mrs. Peabody."

Well, I have always admired Shag's aunt but never
more than at this moment. As I leveled the gun at her, her
old eyes were steady, her massive jaw firm; in fact, she
showed no emotion at all unless it was a slight puzzlement. She was wearing a black silk dress with tiny white
polka dots, a frilled white choker; the steel cane was at
her side, resting on the chair; her hair under the reading
lamp was blue snow.

"Have you really?" she said after a moment. "Well, I
must say that does surprise me. Extraordinary, in fact. So
you've come to murder me, have you? Then perhaps
you'd first do me the favor of explaining why?"

"It's complicated," I said.

"Never mind," said Mrs. Peabody. "Go ahead."

142

I told her about the Contract.

"I see," she said when I had finished. "Well, it doesn't surprise me about young Oliphant. There's no character in that family, you know. That's why San Francisco has never accepted the Oliphants. They're queer. Doesn't matter about poor June's money—the whole lot of them's queer." The word seemed to afford Mrs. Peabody a certain satisfaction. "Not particularly surprised at Shag either—just the sort of idiot thing he'd get involved with. Naturally. But you, Avery—" She was looking at me with great intentness. Her cane fell to the floor. "Pick that up for me, will you? I have trouble stooping at my age."

I hesitated, then approached her chair and picked up the cane and gave it to her.

"Thank you," she said. "Now put that gun on the table there."

I started to obey, but a voice and a sort of drone in my head stopped me. Mrs. Peabody's voice seemed far away. She was saying: "—repeat that! Say it! Quickly!"

"Say what?"

"It's a mental world."

"Say it again."

"It's a mental world."

I did.

"Now say: I'm not going to do anything dreadful to Mrs. Peabody."

I said that—and suddenly the missing part of my mind snapped in. I stared at the gun in my hand and quickly put it on the table near the fruit bowl. I sat down. I stood up. I remembered everything that had happened in the room but just then had no clear idea how or why I happened to be there.

"Look," I said. "I'm *terribly* sorry! Really, I'm—"

"Don't give it a thought," cut in Mrs. Peabody. "You see, I suspected you were hypnotized: I know the signs, thank heaven. Once, when Mr. Peabody was alive, I was attending a house party near Bombay and I saw one of the young consuls hypnotized. Perfect fool did it—a stunt, you see. Then he couldn't manage to get him out of it. Fellow went around the whole weekend thinking he was the Viceroy. Finally I had to. Then when you mentioned Oliphant—did he do it?" Suddenly I remembered.

"Yes."

"Thought so. The whole family's queer. Have an apple."

I took an apple and bit into it; it tasted unusually good.

"That rocket," Mrs. Peabody pursued, "Oliphant's work too?"

"I'm afraid so."

"Does Lavinia realize this as yet?"

"No."

"Well, she mustn't! The shock would probably be too great for her, in her state of health. What about the police?"

I explained that as far as I knew, the police still were working on the theory the rocket was meant for the general.

"And the general's threatening phone calls—Oliphant again?"

"I suppose so," I said. "I hadn't thought of that. But he did say the whole plan was supposed to be foolproof."

"Of course. Let's make a note of that: Oliphant's arrogance. But you say Shag was supposed to—eliminate June Oliphant? How funny! What a thought! But that would naturally be the principal item from young Mr. Oliphant's standpoint, wouldn't it? June Oliphant may not be what you call very rich, but a bird told me she does have a little nest egg of five or six millions and evidently they all go to the nephew, so there you are."

I explained that Warren seemed quite unselfishly interested in the other murders as well, and in fact seemed to take a strange, neurotic pleasure in our complicity in all three.

"I have always avoided thinking about what goes on in a good boys' school," said Mrs. Peabody.

Then, at her request, I helped Mrs. Peabody to her feet and we proceeded to walk around the large room. ("I think best afoot," she told me.) I said that we probably should have gone to the police as soon as Warren showed his hand, but—to my surprise—Mrs. Peabody did not agree.

"When my grandfather came over the Sierras with the miners, Avery, there weren't any police in California worthy of the name. The law was Gold. Naturally, scoundrels were everywhere. So people had to take the law into their own hands: the part of the community with a sense of decency and justice, you see, and something to protect; people of conscience and burning anger. My grandfather was one of these; they were known as the Vigilantes. Oh, of course there were injustices, errors, excesses; people simply love to talk about that part of it. But they forget there was no rule of law then." Mrs. Peabody clenched her fist around her cane and shook it until she almost fell. "Everyone was at the mercy of any thief, murderer, or swindler who wanted to set up shop. We learned to protect ourselves because we had to." We stopped before an immense window and she gestured toward the luminous shape of the Fairmont Towers rising ghostly in the fog. "Look at the city now."

A moment later, I realized that she had lost her place in her thoughts.

"They never should have let them put up the new part of the Fairmont," she said. "Blocks people's views."

I agreed. "I wonder though—about the police: Shag and I thought—"

"Of course, we were talking about the police," she said, stamping her cane. "I was just thinking about that. I was thinking: no, I don't think we should go to the police. Not now. Let's see if we can't deal with Mr. Oliphant ourselves. In the first place, the shock might easily be too much for your aunt. And secondly, it would certainly be all over the paper. Oh, what a perfectly marvelous story for the *Chronicle*. It's got everything—everything but sex, and they'd be dragging that in too somehow, mark my words. Did I tell you what William Randolph Hearst told me once? Of course I did. Take me to the door of my room, Avery; I'm getting tired. You see, it isn't every day a young man of good family whom I've known since he was a small boy calmly enters my apartment and announces he's going to murder me! Don't apologize, I understand perfectly. You weren't yourself. But remember: it's a mental world and you're responsible, no one else. Don't let this Oliphant hypnotize you. If he tries it again, just keep thinking of something definite—like Duty. Second: stay close to your aunt, Avery, at least until I've had a chance to think clearly. When I've done so, I'll be in touch with you." We had progressed to the open door of Mrs. Peabody's bedroom.

"Good night, Avery," she said as she went in and started closing the door. "Take another piece of fruit as you go—also that gun. Otherwise, in the morning my cook will think I've gone coo-coo."

A FATEFUL

DECISION

JOURNEY.—*N*. travel; travelling &c.
v.; wayfaring, campaigning.

journey, excursion, expedition, tour,
trip, grand tour, circuit, peregrination,
discursion, ramble, pilgrimage, course,
ambulation,

plan, itinerary, guide; hand-, road-
book; Bradshaw, Murray.

THE sun was up, burning the fog off the city. As I awoke, I remembered my visit to Mrs. Peabody vaguely and thought it was a nightmare. The foghorns were still going. Then I saw the gun on my desk. I got out of bed and put it in a drawer, then went over to the window expecting to find police surrounding the house, but there was nobody around except the old gardener in dirt-blue Can't-Bust-'ems dragging a hose through the park.

Numbly I got dressed. Apparently I had almost killed Mrs. Peabody. I remembered the gyrating, pulsing lights and Warren's voice—

Suddenly I knew what I had to do.

I found her at breakfast on the sunny loggia talking to the Princess on her Princess telephone. A freighter was moving into a fog bank under the Golden Gate Bridge. The Hawaiian Islands, I thought; Aunt Lavinia likes the

Hawaiian Islands. She gets on well with my mother and my stepfather and their rather conservative circle of pineapple ranchers and retired warriors. Perhaps we would continue on to Tokyo, Hong Kong and around the world again—anything to get as far away from Warren as possible!

The *Chronicle* was on the table, and as I sat down I took it and scanned the front page to see if, by any chance, Mrs. Peabody hadn't, after all—but of course she hadn't. However, at the bottom there was a boxed feature with Connie Beasy's by-line headed "Socialite at Home After Blast," which I had just begun to read when I heard Aunt Lavinia saying:

"—and of course Witter's against my going at all. He says the numbers aren't right. You know. He says it isn't safe. But you know Witter. And Dotty Rodney said she had a perfectly lovely time. Yes. She said it was completely different from any experience she'd ever had before. Those were her exact words." She looked at me and then said, "Oh, I think he will—after all, it's only while Freddie's doing the living room and— What? Oh, no, it's going to be all lovely shades of jade and apricot."

We were traveling again.

At that moment, I felt considerable relief. I saw us jetting to some peaceful spa far from Warren, where I could think. Then she hung up and I found out where she had decided to go.

"We can't," I said.

"Why not? But of course we can. Everyone's going there now. And Dotty says that place called Paradise Roc is perfectly lovely and very comfortable. What's the matter, Avery? Of course, if you'd prefer not to go with me—"

I assured her that I wanted to accompany her but urged that we go anywhere else, anywhere. I proposed Hawaii, Japan, Europe. I proposed any other Caribbean resort—Barbados, the Virgin Islands, Jamaica. I suggested Rio, Tangiers, London. But no place in the world seemed to beckon my aunt just then except, by some fateful mischance, the primitive island republic with its voodoo and unsavory politics which was the headquarters of Warren's operations!

Saint Sebastian.

"As a matter of fact," said Aunt Lavinia, having dismissed all my entreaties, "you gave me the idea yourself."

"*I* did?"

"Yes. You mentioned Saint Sebastian when we were in Greece—the day we went to the Parthenon. Oh, come along, Avery. It should be very amusing. In fact, I think it will be different from any experience we've ever had before!"

There was nothing to be done. By ill chance, Aunt Lavinia's travel woman was able to book us on a Pan Am flight for San Juan the very next morning and from there, after two days at the Hotel San Juan, to Saint Sebastian. The Paradise Roc Beach Club. It was all settled by ten o'clock. In a state of depression, I went to the library and called Timberline at Freddie's.

153

She was there—that is, she was there physically, but as
far as I was concerned she might have been in Green-
land.

"How nice," she said, when I had told her about the
new trip. "Have a perfectly lovely time."

"But I have to stay near her," I said, "especially down
there."

"Of course you do," she said, adding before she hung
up: "Just watch out for traps."

THE MAGIC

ISLAND

431. BLACKNESS.—*N.* blackness &c.
adj.; darkness &c. (*want of light*) 421;
swarthness, lividity, dark colour, tone,
colour; *chiaroscuro* &c. 420.

nigrification, infuscation.

jet, ink, ebony, coal, pitch, soot,
charcoal, sloe, smut, raven, crow;
negro, blackamoor, man of colour, nig-
ger, darkie, Ethiop, black.

Adj. black, sable, swarthy, sombre,
dark, inky, ebon, atramentous, jetty;
coal-, jet-black; fuliginous, pitchy,
sooty, swart, dusky, dingy, murky,
Ethiopic; low-toned, low in tone; of
the deepest dye.

black as -jet &c. *n.*, – my hat, – a
shoe, – a tinker's pot, – November, –
thunder, – midnight; nocturnal &c.
(*dark*) 421; nigrescent; obscure &c.
421.

Adv. in mourning.

SAINT SEBASTIAN, "The Magic Island of the Caribbean," is a former French colony, for two hundred years an independent Negro republic; population: 3,000,000; religions: Roman Catholic and Dahomey Voodoo; languages: officially French, popularly Creole; capital: Porte Sebastian; principal industries: rum, sisal, mahogany, luxury tourism, gambling; national sport: cockfighting; head of state: Dr. Alphonse Hermoso, ex-barber, voodoo houngan, dictator. From the moment our Viscount's wheels touched down on the Saint Sebastian "International" Airport, I felt an ominous peculiarity about the place. Definitely.

As we left the plane, the sun hung low over the end of the runway, and in the reddish light a lot of Saint Sebastians stood around the pocked-stucco terminal building casting daddy-long-legs shadows on the tarmac. There was a penetrating smell of kerosene and something I couldn't identify. Kee-kee, in my aunt's arms, seemed intimidated by the presence of so many independent

Negro people all at once. Under a huge billboard, a motley orchestra of a half-dozen ragged boys with big bamboo tubes, tin horns, and a drum struck up a calliope-like march, apparently the national anthem. The sign, mounted on a high, barbed-wire-topped fence separating the arrival area from the rutted parking area behind the terminal and customs shed, was a WPA-style mural depicting laborers, women carrying baskets on their heads, children, sugar-cane fields, sunbeams, and in the center of it all a scholarly looking man wearing glasses and what appeared to be a cement business suit. Underneath was the legend:

JE SUIS LE DRAPEAU
Hermoso

The sign dwarfed the musicians below it.

"What is 'drapeau'?" asked Aunt Lavinia, as we reached the bottom of the stairs from the plane. "I know the word but I can't remember what it means."

" 'Flag,' " I told her.

" 'I am the flag,' " she translated, then: "How interesting."

Just then we heard a shrill voice behind us calling her name. I turned and, among the other de-planing passengers, identified a Mrs. Herman Quigley, a widowed San Francisco lady of my aunt's general coloration and bracket, making her way down the stairs toward us, among the blacks, as if each step that separated us was an absurd prank of fate.

"Lavinia!"

"Isobel!"

I shall not evoke in detail the little drama that happens whenever two San Francisco ladies encounter on some barbarous shore: the wonderment, the unbelieving delight, though they may be barely on nodding terms at home. Even some of the Saint Sebastians around us, doubtless accustomed to strong feelings themselves, were impressed. It developed that Mrs. Quigley had not seen us on the airplane and neither had we seen Mrs. Quigley, and by way of further coincidence, we were all staying at the same place—the Paradise Roc Beach Club. As we approached the customs shed to the cacophonous yet strangely insinuating accompaniment of the little orchestra, a single-engined jet, which I identified later as an F-86 belonging to the Saint Sebastian Air Force, loafed over about fifty or sixty feet above our heads, partially defoliating a mimosa tree. Mrs. Quigley made a wry face, but no fracas could upset the ladies' joyous reunion. When my ears partially cleared, I heard Kee-kee, in Aunt Lavinia's arms, barking: on a bench near the customs area, an enormous mastiff was being patted and restrained by two men in combat dress, bulbous blue helmets, and large eyeglasses which were not merely dark but black. The men smiled at us. Like dog lovers everywhere. I realized suddenly they were members of Dr. Hermoso's finest, the curiously efficient special police locally known as Boom-booms. Their presence seemed to reassure the ladies and Mrs. Quigley remembered that she had read somewhere there were no Communists on Saint Sebastian.

Through customs we were met by a stocky, expeditious man with a cap inscribed "Paradise Roc" who rounded up our luggage and guided us to a much-shined Cadillac limousine dating from the McCarthy period. My aunt and Mrs. Quigley got in back, talking. I started to get in the front seat next to the driver, wanting to learn whatever I could about Warren's adoptive home, when from the jungle far across the runway I heard a lazy crepitation that sounded like machine-gun fire. I got in, looking inquiringly at the driver as he started the car. It seemed to need service.

"Fiesta," he said finally, as we took off in a swerve through the parking area. "We have fiesta now in Saint Sebastian."

The road was full of potholes and in the tarpaper settlements crowded with raggedly dressed people, dogs, pigs, chickens, out for the cool of the evening. Our driver showed no apparent concern for the lives of his countrymen, for whenever the road ahead looked solidly blocked with people and minor livestock, he leaned on the horn, speeded up, and shot through the mélée spraying chickens right and left but miraculously not hitting anyone. It was quite exhilarating.

Beyond the villages stringing out from the airport, the road climbed through sugar-cane fields before dropping again toward the ramshackle outskirts of Porte Sebastian. On our right, in one of the fields, still touched by the sun, I saw a curious sight: a group of ten or a dozen men in scarecrow clothes were mechanically chopping sugar cane. The laborers looked odd. Very odd. In fact, they looked unwell. Their faces were off-white and their movements unnatural. Some wore rags tied around their heads, straw hats.

"More fiesta?" I said to the driver.

"No, sah," he said, in a Wurlitzer voice pitched so my aunt and Mrs. Quigley would not hear. "Zombies."

The Paradise Roc Beach Club (known to its regulars as "The Rock") is situated above its own sheltered cove on the cape that forms the northwest tip of the island. It is English-owned, Chicago-designed, French-managed, French-chefed, Saint Sebastian-staffed, and for the most part American-occupied. The rates are a democratic $1,000 per guest per week including snorkling lessons, the use of a chauffeured car and free admission to the Porte Sebastian Casino and its high-stake card rooms. One lodges in a suite in the main building or, as Aunt Lavinia's and my reservation indicated, one of the cottages in the tropical gardens surrounding the hotel.

The device

in the iron gates signals one's arrival at this Xanadu. One drives up a cobbled horseshoe road that climbs through the gardens concealing the hotel from the gates. At the hour of our arrival, birds were chirruping and whirring in the last sunbursts in the tops of the royal palms; saffron finches,

banana quits, birds like that. The perfume of bougainvillea, jasmine was overpowering, narcotic. Through the
darkening trees and shrubbery I glimpsed lanterns, heard
faint marimba music.

"Well, here we are," said Mrs. Quigley. "It looks
charming."

"Yes, doesn't it," said Aunt Lavinia. "I think it's going
to be quite fun."

Yes.

The manager, Monsieur Poulet (prenom: Eustache),
was a lean, restless, affairé Frenchman who seemed com-
forted—if only momentarily—by my aunt's and Mrs.
Quigley's obvious wealth. About me, he seemed more
doubtful. We registered. Monsieur Poulet snapped his
fingers and dispatched Mrs. Quigley with the assistant
manager and boy to her rooms in the hotel proper. Aunt
Lavinia and me he took in personal charge, and followed
by two boys with our bags and a maid we set forth,
spiritoso, for our cottage.

As we passed through it, the doors in the main common room were open onto a lantern-lit, pink-umbrellaed
terrace, where the marimba band was entertaining tables
of guests. Beyond the terrace: a colonnaded pavilion of
pink marble and beyond the pavilion a vast lawn extending to the sunset. It was all as advertised.

Even the big man seemed to fit into the scene.

This portly and impressive-looking individual sat at the
table nearest the doors, watching us as we passed through

the common room. He was a florid, vigorous-looking person of about sixty, blue blazer, yellow shirt, yellow ascot, looking at us with an intense hawk-like stare.

Our cottage was a modern two-bedroom affair with a central sitting room done in a mixture of Caribbean Primitive—wooden masks, native painting, mahogany artifacts —and Contemporary Industrial Design—wall-to-wall synthetics, sidereal wallpaper, perforated light fixtures. Aunt Lavinia seemed to like it. I stepped out on the porch to investigate the strategic defenses, found the cottage was closed in on all sides by the Chicago-lit gardens. The hotel swimming pool, lighted and visible through a break in the trees, was unoccupied and placid, like a giant lemon drop. I listened. Faintly, under the music and voices from the hotel, the chattering of birds, I heard the sound of surf on the north shore and, still more faintly but, once heard, persistently, the beat of voodoo drums.

As I stepped back into the sitting room, the lights went out. In the half-light of the afterglow outside, Monsieur Poulet issued crisp orders for candles and lamps.

"Blackout," he explained. "Do not wor-ry. It happens almost every night and will last no more than an hour."

"Why?" I asked.

"A question of—economics, Monsieur."

"The hotel's?"

"Certainly not! The government. The whole country is now without electricity—except, of course, the President's palace and the Casino."

"Of course."

"I would think, Monsieur," said Aunt Lavinia, "they could leave the electricity on during the fiesta."

At first the manager looked at her blankly, then:

"Fiesta! Yes, of course. This is what some people call the—life here. Fiesta. Yes. Now, shall I show you the bedroom?"

Just at that moment, however, there was a sharp scream from the bedroom and the maid came out. She stopped, looked once at Aunt Lavinia, then sped past us and disappeared out the door and into the gardens. The two bag carriers then appeared, walking, not running, but definitely leaving. The manager shouted something in Creole after them, apologized to Aunt Lavinia, went into the bedroom and came out again. It was a single maneuver. He closed the door behind him.

"It is nothing," he announced, turning pale.

Two charred sticks tied together with a dirty piece of red ribbon had caused all the fuss. I found this strange talisman on one of the pillows of the half-turned-down bed destined for Aunt Lavinia, who came in and saw it too.

"What is that, Avery?" she asked me.

"I don't know," I told her. "A trick perhaps. Probably nothing."

"But who would ever want to play a trick on me?"

"True," I said. "Perhaps it's really a trick on the manager. Let's ask him."

Back in the sitting room, we found Monsieur Poulet seated talking to himself in French. I caught the word "Perpignan." He stood up quickly when we came in.

"Monsieur Poulet!" I said in a peremptory tone. "What is the meaning of this object? Is this someone's idea of a joke?"

To his credit, Poulet steadied himself at once. He took a breath and said, "That is what they call in voodoo an ouanga. Sometimes—like the—Saint Christophe—it can mean no harm comes to you. It can mean—many things."

"But why did everyone run out of the room, Monsieur?" asked my aunt.

"Superstition, Madame," he said, all manager again. "I do not understand the voodoo, so I cannot tell you. It's a religion, quoi. The day after tomor-row we will have for you a voodoo show here at the hotel. Un petit spectacle, n'est-ce pas. Most of the guests find it most interesting. Now, if you wish, I can give you a suite in the hotel, near Mrs. Quig-ley."

I was for making the change but Aunt Lavinia would not hear of it. She said we weren't superstitious. When she retired to her room, I caught up with the manager on his way out the door.

"This isn't a Saint Christopher, is it?" I said.

"No, Monsieur," he told me. "It was a mistake. Do not be concerned."

"How do you know it was a mistake?" He looked at me a moment. No love lost.

"Because you and your aunt are tourists and the law now against harming a tourist is severe. *Very* severe. Besides, your aunt can have no enemies in Saint Sebastian. It was a mistake, of course."

We looked at each other. We were both holding back. A few birdcalls later, I said:

"That voodoo show you mentioned—that wouldn't be Mr. Oliphant's troupe, by any chance?"

The manager's expression didn't change. At all. I could guess he was busy trying to figure if I still fitted the Dumb but Harmless American Tourist category.

"Oui, monsieur," he said warily. "It is Mr. Oliphant's troupe."

"Thought they were touring the States?"

"They have returned—yesterday. Then you saw the performance in the States?"

"Yes. San Francisco. Quite good."

The manager's nerves seemed to slacken off a bit. On an impulse, I stuck the ouanga in the upper pocket of his vanilla-colored jacket. He stiffened again. We said good night correctly, but just. When he had gone, I experienced an odd sense of exhilaration, battle readiness. Warren was already back on Saint Sebastian.

En garde!

I realized that somehow I must have known it from the moment we set foot on these magical shores only one hour earlier.

CONTACTS

290. [Motion nearer to.] CONVER-GENCE.—*N.* con-vergence, -fluence, -course, -flux, -gress, -currence, -centration; appulse, meeting; corradiation.

assemblage &c. 72; resort &c. (*focus*) 74; asymptote.

V. converge, concur; come together, unite, meet, fall in with; close -with, – in upon; centre -round, – in; enter in; pour in.

gather together, unite, concentrate, bring into a focus.

Adj. converging &c. *v.*; convergent, -fluent, -current; centripetal; asymptotical.

THAT night I slept fitfully. Toward morning, I dreamed of the stone fragment falling from the Parthenon—except it wasn't falling: it was just hanging there in mid-air giving me time to save Aunt Lavinia; only I couldn't run: my legs were free but they wouldn't move. I awoke sweating, dozed off again. It was almost ten o'clock when I finally got up. Martes.

A note on the breakfast table on the porch informed me that Aunt Lavinia was spending the morning with Mrs. Quigley touring Porte Sebastian. There was a second communication on the table, this one in a sealed blue envelope with my name penned in a back-slanting hand. The note inside was curt and to the point:

At the pool. 11:00.

No signature.

After breakfast, I walked up through the warbling gardens to ask for mail at the desk, hoping for a letter or a communication from Shag. The assistant manager told me there was nothing, the mail came later in the morning. Leaving the desk, I noticed the lithographed announcement on the bulletin board:

CARIBE COCKTAIL
authentic voodoo
calypso
SUNDAY   6 PM
The Paradise Roc Beach Club

It was only then that I realized who had sent the note.

I found a vacant lounging chair by the side of the pool facing the sun. 10:50. There were already a dozen or so other guests lying on the long, reclining chairs or sitting at tables under pink umbrellas; some of them were watching the Negro lifeguard walking on his hands by the edge of the water. A radio was playing Latin music. It was a fairly typical crowd for a place like Paradise Roc: chic, weather-beaten, a trifle leathery. Several American women in dressmaker bathing suits, careful hair sets, were stretched out flat on lounge chairs with cotton balls in their eyes. There was a young couple, big, squarely built people who kept whispering to each other, then laughing helplessly. I recognized the same silver-bronze industrialist I had seen at the Athens pool with the girl rubbing oil into his back—only this time it was a different girl. Across the pool, a woman was sitting at a table grimly writing post card after post card, while her censorious-looking husband, in a lounge chair, watched the Negro lifeguard, who now tipped upright on his feet and began dancing with a dark-haired girl with a deep tan and a pockmarked face. Several people were in the pool, swimming or standing.

Then, at the farthest table across the pool, I noticed the big hawk-eyed man I had seen on the terrace the night before, watching me.

I settled back on the hot canvas of the chair and let the sun hit me. Overhead in the bougainvillea, palms and pines of the gardens, the birds suddenly set up a screeching like the sound track of an old Dorothy Lamour film. From somewhere I heard the doleful talk of voodoo drums and below the hotel grounds, on the north shore, the faint sizzle of the sea on a pebble beach. I felt an unaccountable peace. It didn't last.

I had opened my eyes the merest slit to see if the big man was still watching me (he was), when I noticed a girl swimming directly toward me underwater. I knew who it was even before she popped up at the edge of the pool. Shill.

"Surprised?" she said.

"Not too," I told her. "I got your note."

Water reflections bobbed on her face, then her smile came on, hard but not cold. She looked at me for a moment, then hoisted herself out of the water. I observed she was wearing a green bikini that in most places would be a statutory misdemeanor. Haloed, she stood directly in the sun and pulled her cap off, letting her hair spill out, shook it loose, then stretched out on her stomach on the lounge chair next to me; she smelled nicely of almonds and lanolin. The big man watched her. The censorious man watched her too, furtively fascinated.

"You don't sound very glad to see me," she said, "but then I suppose by now I'm just a harbinger to you, or something."

"What do you expect?" I said. "Every time you turn up, something dreadful happens."

"It's not my fault."

"Your friend sent you this time too, I suppose?"

Her long fingers drew lines from a water puddle on the concrete. "Yes and no," she said after a moment, then: "Listen, if you weren't so far-offish, I might be able to do something for you—if you want something done, that is."

"Far-offish!" I said. "Look. Of course, I want something done, but who was it who sent me off on a wild-goose chase the night Aunt Lavinia was almost killed? And then who—"

"Warren," she said. "But—a wild-goose chase—I thought you liked Miss Green Eyes."

"I *do*, but—"

Shill frowned in annoyance. "Do you think I would have sent you over there if it was—if I could help it? To Green Eyes? That was his idea. Can't you understand? That was for my benefit."

"But, Shill," I said experimentally, "you certainly don't

have to do everything Warren tells you. You're free, white and—what? Twenty?"

"Twenty-one."

"Not married to him, are you?"

She just laughed, then she said:

"Avery, do you believe in legends? And don't say some of them."

"Some of them."

"Tell me!" she insisted. The censorious man and his wife were both staring at her; she made a face at them.

"You mean dragons and heroes and fair ladies and—"

"—and spells and enchantments—and quests. Do you?"

"As stories, of course, but—"

"Oh, Avery," she said with apparently genuine exasperation. *"Use your imagination!* What do you think I'm trying to tell you?"

"Who discovered America?" I asked her suddenly.

"Leif Ericson."

"The next time?"

"Columbus."

"States in the Union?"

"Fifty."

"Westernmost?"

"Alaska."

"What are you trying to tell me?"

She started to say something but bit her lip. She seemed to want to say it but couldn't.

"Do you stay here at the hotel?" I asked her at last.

"No," she said. "Pool privileges. I have all sorts of privileges on this lousy island. I live at his house."

"Warren must be a big man here."

"He is." She rolled over and closed her eyes against the sun. "Very big. But not so big as he thinks." A minute later: "Avery."

"Yes."

"Why did you bring your aunt here?"

"I didn't," I said. "She wanted to come here. I tried to have her go somewhere else, but—"

"You don't have to insist," she said, still with her eyes closed.

Just then I heard a hissing sound in the gardens to my left, beyond the deep end of the pool.

"Mister, Mister!"

I looked. A little Saint Sebastian boy standing half concealed behind the trunk of a palm stepped out and held up a wooden mask. I started to look away.

"Mister!" he said again, urgently. Now he had some strings of beads. I saw that he was wearing only a lot of red cock-feathers around his middle. Just as I turned away again, he began churning his little fanny like an egg-beater.

Shill went on as if she hadn't noticed:

"And so anyway, here you are in Saint Sebastian with Aunt Lavinia—and you don't want the Contract to happen?"

"Absolutely not." She rolled on her side and leaned her head on her hand, looking at me.

A new sort of communication began between us. I watched an oily water drop travel down her tanned neck until it broke on the white frontier of her bikinied breast.

174

After a few moments, she looked across the pool where something had caught her attention.

"Want to see something funny?"

Reluctantly I followed her glance. In a locust-like tree spreading out over the pink umbrellas, a big iguana was edging perilously far out on the slender branches toward a cluster of blossoms.

"That iguana is perfectly harmless," Shill commentated in a low voice, "and actually quite timid. They eat flowers. Only over there the flowers are just too far out but Mr. Iguana doesn't care about that. He probably thinks he's still a little baby iguana anyway. Ooo, look—"

The reptile had lost its footing on the branches and after a half-hearted attempt to catch itself fell placidly to the cement near the censorious man and his wife. The wife screamed and there was a chair-tipping scramble as the man frantically kiddie-carred his chair backwards. The sun-communicants were sitting up clutching the tops of their bathing suits, watching the event. The big man at the other table, I noticed, was watching Shill and me the whole time. The lifeguard came over to the frightened couple but the iguana had already waddled into the gardens. Shill turned her back on the scene.

"I notice you always seem to be on the monster's side," I said.

"Very perceptive," she said. "I guess I always have. At least I always used to be. No, I don't know any more. When I was a little girl, I was always more fascinated by the dragons and Minotaurs and Merlins than by the Lancelots. That was why I took up with Warren, I guess. I wanted to see how the world looked from the monster side. Can you understand that?"

"I think so, but it sounds sort of frivolous."

"There was more to it," she went on, paying little attention to me, as if she was figuring these things out for the first time. "And besides, I had this idea that—I wanted to slay monsters myself. Not like Lancelot or Theseus with a sword or anything but—in my own way."

"Like a girl."

Shill smiled.

"Only it didn't work out that way," I suggested.

"No, it didn't," she said with sudden bitterness. "I joined the C.I.A.—did you know it's very difficult for a girl to join the C.I.A.? Well, it is. Damned difficult. I was at the University of Michigan then. God, how I want to go back to the University of Michigan!"

"I didn't know you were in the C.I.A.," I said.

"I'm not. Not any more. They sent me down here—I should say they sent me out in the 'field,' and in the 'field' I met your charming school friend, in the line of duty, too. And it wasn't very long until I'd 'lost my usefulness,' as they say. Definitely."

"You found your monster?"

"Let's just say I can understand now why they don't like girls in the C.I.A."

"But now if you want to leave Warren and go back to Michigan, why don't you?"

Shill was silent a moment; then, as she was about to answer something, I saw her eyes suddenly raise slightly and I caught a movement in them. I looked around just

176

as a shiny black Porsche pulled into a turn-out in the horseshoe drive near the pool and stopped, motor running. Reflections of overhanging trees, sky, birds in the windshield prevented my seeing the driver. The parking lights went on, then off, twice.

"I'm not even supposed to be seen talking to you," said Shill in a dull voice, slowly getting up from the chair.

"Is that Warren?"

She nodded, then: "Meet me here at eleven-thirty tonight."

"Wait," I said, "I'm going over to have a few words with him."

"No!" she said sharply. "Meet me here at eleven-thirty." When I hesitated, she added: "You do want the Contract, don't you?"

I thought: Shag didn't get it back!

Then without waiting for an answer, she grabbed her cap and ran over to the car (an illogical girl-run displaying breath-taking rear cleavage), got in and slammed the door. The Porsche backed into the drive, then shot down the cobbles toward the hotel gates. I caught one glimpse of Warren as he passed, looking directly at me.

A few of the guests had noticed Shill's sudden departure, including the big man.

ENTER

LORD BOBBY

875. NOBILITY.—*N.* nobility, rank, condition, distinction, optimacy, blood, *pur sang*, birth, high descent, order; quality, gentility.

high life, *haut monde*; upper -classes, – ten thousand; *elite,* aristocracy, great folks; fashionable world &c. (*fashion*) 852.

peer, -age; house of -lords, – peers; lords, *noblesse*; noble, -man; lord, -ling; grandee, *magnifico, hidalgo*; don, -ship; aristocrat, swell, three-tailed bashaw; gentleman, squire, squireen, patrician, boyar, margrave, vavasour, emir, ameer, scherif, effendi, sahib.

personage –, man- of -distinction, – mark, – rank; big-wig, magnate, great man, star; *magni nominis umbra.*

Adj. noble, exalted; of -rank &c. *n.*; titled, patrician, aristocratic; high-, well-born; of gentle blood; genteel, *comme il faut,* gentlemanlike, courtly &c. (*fashionable*) 852; highly respectable.

Adv. in high quarters.

MINUTES must have passed: I opened my eyes and found him standing in the sun. He indicated the lounging chair Shill had just vacated.

"Good morning. May I?"

I added an ultra-U British accent to my portrait of the big man, noticing that his hawkish aspect was due to great tufted eyebrows upswept at the ends and quick steely blue eyes, oddly out of match with his jowly lower face.

"Of course," I said.

He sat down on the side of the lounging chair and fixed me with a look of fierce geniality. He wore blue madras walking shorts, a cream-colored sport shirt, Jasak Phillipe wrist watch and, behind his ear, an unobtrusive plastic hearing aid, the wire of which I traced to his shirt pocket.

"Robert Twitchell," he offered.

"Avery Ashley."

"I know, sir. Made inquiries of the manager after your

181

arrival last night with the two ladies, your aunt and Mrs. Quiggins."

"Quigley."

"Quigley, of course. From San Francisco."

"Yes."

"As you yourself, sir, and Mrs. Vigorex."

"That's right." I settled back and closed my eyes. Several seconds of bird song and marimba elapsed, then:

"Mr. Ashley, aren't you even going to ask my *why* I asked about you and your party last evening?"

"I was," I said, "until I decided you were going to tell me anyway."

"Ho!" he said, swinging his legs up and settling back in the chair as if everything was going to be just dandy from now on. "Jolly good. And I will tell you: It was simple curiosity. What do you say to that? Go ahead."

"On behalf of my party and me," I said, "we're flattered."

"Good. *Very* good." (I was soon to understand that my new acquaintance had a disconcerting way, sometimes, of presenting bouquets for one's conversational efforts instead of replies.) "Now, sir, I want to tell you something else, if I may?"

"Go ahead."

"I want to tell you what brought me over here to introduce myself to you against all rules of accepted behavior."

"Simple curiosity?"

"Not quite. Not quite, this time. I came to ask you

if you knew that charming girl you were just talking to, before?"

"Slightly."

"Strikingly attractive young person."

"Yes."

"And the chap she drove off with?" He said it casually but something told me that the "chap" interested him at least as much as the "strikingly attractive young person." My brain was flashing a red alert as I said evenly:

"I think he's a friend of hers."

My answer obviously disappointed him.

"You know nothing at all about him?"

"No. Do you?"

His voice dropped a key as he said, "I'll be more candid than I believe you are being, Mr. Ashley. I'll say, yes. I'll say, I do know something about him. I'll even say that I know his name is Warren Oliphant."

As he said Warren's name, I felt him studying the left side of my face. I remember hearing the crazy laughter of the hysterical couple.

"What makes you think I know him?" I said finally.

"For one thing," said Robert Twitchell, "I observed you were about to go over and speak to him—until the girl dissuaded you."

"You're a pretty good observer. What else?"

"Well, there is the fact that you arrived in this rather out-of-the-way place with your aunt and Mrs.—"

"Quigley."

"Quigley—only twenty-four hours after Mr. Oliphant

and the girl you were talking to and Mr. Oliphant's peripatetic voodoo troupe, and the further fact that both parties arrived from the same place of origin. Oh, yes, of course, observations of this sort are only as good as one's assessments of them, aren't they? But ah, San Francisco! What a delightful and fascinating city—though I'm afraid for myself if I lived there, I should quickly perish from overconsumption of your Dungeness crab."

"Mr. Twitchell," I said, "may I ask what your interest is in—the man in the car?"

"Of course you can, dear fellow, except for the moment— But look, isn't it your aunt and Mrs.—Quigley returning from their morning outing?"

In fact, at the head of the drive, Aunt Lavinia and Mrs. Quigley were alighting from the Cadillac, with Kee-kee and packages. Both ladies were wearing vibrant prismatic frocks and had acquired large hats of woven sisal with the ends left frayed in abandoned haloes. Instead of entering the hotel, they started down the path following the curve of the drive, toward us.

"They're coming our way," said Twitchell with every appearance of pleasure. "Perhaps, Mr. Ashley, you'd be good enough to introduce me. It's Robert Twitchell—but people generally call me Lord Bobby."

So that was how Lord Bobby entered the picture. Aunt Lavinia invited him to join us for lunch, while Mrs. Quigley fell into the state of almost cataleptic obeisance which I've noticed attacks some San Francisco ladies

184

when suddenly thrust into the presence of British aristocracy. Aunt Lavinia and Lord Bobby kept pace with
each other in an exhilarating run through the fields of
international society, dropping "Ci-ci's" and "Nonies"
and "His Grace's" and "Baron Guy's" until Mrs. Quigley was quite spellbound and affected. Meanwhile
through the lunch, during which he and I frequently
paused to reconnoiter each other's faces, it became clear
that Lord Bobby's attendance on the ladies (particularly
on Aunt Lavinia) was not to terminate with the meal. He
proposed that we try our luck at the Casino that evening.
When this suggestion was promptly accepted, he then advanced plans for an excursion the next morning on the
bay in a glass-bottomed boat. Lord Bobby was clearly
with us—but was he, I wondered, too much with us? A
boy brought me a letter on a mahogany tray and I managed to slip it into my jacket pocket before Aunt Lavinia
noticed the familiar aquamarine of the Frobisher and
Frobisher envelope.

Lord Bobby, of course, did notice.

Fifteen minutes later, when we had parted for siestas,
I made the discovery that Lord Bobby's cottage was the
nearest one to our own and, as it turned out, visible from
our terrace when the afternoon trade winds parted the
palms in a certain way. As I heard Aunt Lavinia drawing
her curtains, he appeared briefly on his terrace and waved
genially before the trees shut him from view. I tore open
Shag's letter, still wondering who the big Englishman
was and what might account for his interest in Warren.

A LETTER

FROM SHAG

532. NEWS.—*N*. news; information &c. 527; piece –, budget- of -news, – information; intelligence, tidings.

word, advice, *aviso,* message; dis-, des-patch; telegram, communication, errand, embassy; *bulletin.*

fresh –, stirring –, old –, stale-news; glad tidings; old –, stale-story.

V. transpire &c. (*be disclosed*)

D_{EAR} A_{VE},

The following will acquaint you with the notable events of Tuesday night.

9:30 Park on Laguna St. hill below house, careful to turn wheels into curb as required by law. Check equipment: flashlight, key to back door (supplied by Warren), Woolworth bat mask.

9:32 Leave car. Approach house. Noisy group leaving party across the street. Pass house and return when noisy group disperses. Don bat mask.

9:36 Start up alley. Hear sounds from within: TV gunfire, stampede. Try key in back door. Door opens easily. Odd feeling of nonparticipation. Enter. Switch on flashlight. Cross rapidly to gun-room door. Find door unlocked. Enter. Discover everything—packing crates, rocket launcher, other ordnance, files, everything—gone! No trace. Only guns in glass cases left. Everything clean as a whistle. No Contract.

9:39 Leave gun room. Start up cellar stairs. (Can't

exactly account for this move except as conditioned re-
flex due to having left by stairs and front door on pre-
vious visit, plus nervous tension.) Stair creaks. Hear TV.
Turn and descend stairs. Halfway to door when TV is
suddenly louder and light wedge appears on concrete
floor. Aunt June. Following conversation ensues:

She: Who's there?

Me:

She: Is that you, Bunny? Don't try to scare me.

Me:

She (louder): Bunny, is that you?

Me: Yes. Go to bed, Auntie.

She:

Me:

She: You aren't Bunny. Who are you?

Me (after pause): The Bat Burglar.

She: Bunny—it is you, isn't it?

Me: Yes.

At this point, however, she realizes I am not Warren,
and as I rush for the outside door, she has one of the
main-floor windows on the street side open and is yelling
"Bat Burglar! Bat Burglar!" Somehow, I make it to the
car and get away. Undetected, I think. I am not certain.
It is always possible that someone, possibly Aunt June
herself, recognized me and that the police are even
now outside my door. I live with this possibility day and
night.

Ave, I am not blaming you—my signature on that
idiotic document is graphic proof that I was as naive

about Warren as you were—but now, besides my very real apprehensions about being arrested, I open the *Chronicle* every morning with the expectation of reading that Aunt Lavinia has been assassinated in Saint Sebastian! Couldn't you have done something to deter her from safari-ing on precisely *that* island? I know you are not collaborating (at least consciously) in Warren's psychotic enterprises but the moment has definitely come to ACT—NOW!— GET AUNT LAVINIA OFF THAT ISLAND!

I saw him Wednesday. Yes, on the very morning of my abortive adventure in housebreaking, I was summoned to the Hawk Club by that weird girl of his. Ave, it was a very unsettling experience. Warren is definitely off the deep end and I was positive he was leaving San Francisco with the definite intention of finishing his part of the Contract in Saint Sebastian! So, friend, it is up to you. Above all, you should have nothing to do with that girl called Shill, as should be obvious. I only mention this because in the past, you have sometimes demonstrated astonishing suspensions of insight when confronted with exotic females (i.e., those who present themselves to you as such). There is no question at all of the girl's nubility but this should hardly be your uppermost consideration just at the moment. Verbum sap.

As for Aunt Christine, time will tell if it was advisable to tell her about the Contract but the revelation has hardly enhanced my own standing with her. Paradoxically she seems to bear no grudge against you for almost assassinating her (in fact, she even said the experience "stimulated" her) but I am meanwhile cast in the role of feeble tool. Fortunately, she still feels that the police should not be brought in because of the publicity and that Aunt Lavinia should not be told because of the danger to her health. She thinks Warren can be dealt with and, oddly, has faith in you in spite of what happened. She also says to tell you that reinforcements are on the way. What she means by this I have no idea and she won't explain. I somehow got the idea the old girl was thinking of going down there herself, but when I questioned her, she said, "Dear boy, the first flight I make by air will be through the Pearly Gates." So be ready for anything.

Shag

P.S.   Aunt Christine has taken a great liking to that artist-friend of yours, Timberline, and took her to the Symphony last Thursday, which, as you well know, is the ultimate accolade.

I put the letter back in my pocket and went out on the porch, where, though alone, I was not unobserved. Below in the gardens, the little red-feathered boy was waiting; when I looked down, he called, "Mister! Mister!", held out an open palm and waggled his rear end optimistically. I adopted an attitude of amused indulgence and looked away. Through the palms lazily flailing in the hot afternoon breezes, I caught a glimpse of Lord Bobby on the porch of his cottage, which was about seventy-five yards distant; he waved to me just as the trees closed again. Inside, I heard Aunt Lavinia's mystery story fall to the floor. I took out Shag's letter and read until I came to the part that troubled me:

"... start up cellar stairs ..."

Why had Shag started up the cellar stairs?

I spent the rest of that torrid afternoon at the pool with my thoughts.

AU CASINO

621. [Absence of purpose in the succession of events.] CHANCE. † —N. chance &c. 156; lot, fate &c. (*necessity*) 601; luck; good luck &c. (*good*) 618.

game of chance; mere –, random-shot; blind bargain, leap in the dark (*uncertainty*) 475; fluke, pot-luck.

sortes. – *Virgilianæ; rouge et noir,* hazard, *roulette,* pitch and toss, chuck-farthing, cup-tossing, heads or tails, cross and pile, wager; bet, -ting; gambling; the turf.

gaming-, gambling-, betting-house; hell; betting ring; dice, – box; dicer; gam-bler, -ester.

HAT evening at nine, after a festive dinner à quatre at the hotel, Aunt Lavinia, Mrs. Quigley, Lord Bobby and I alighted from the hotel Cadillac before the Saint Sebastian International Casino, which, as a connoisseur of casinos, I immediately awarded three stars for the sort of unwholesome panache one expects of these places. It is a sprawling one-story structure of leprous stucco, with balustraded cornices and great tall windows flanked by fluted extrusions and surmounting scallop-shell balconies. Most of the windows have been blown by hurricanes and boarded up. The whole edifice is built on piles and there is the wreckage of a boat pier staggering out into the moonlit bay.

Inside, past the desk where they issue admission cards, one enters a large room clicking with roulette balls and craps dice. Already there were quite a few people at the tables, sitting silently in smoky cones of light from the hanging green-shaded lamps: a mixed lot of Saint Sebastians of the better sort, tourists and members of the small community of foreign émigrés of the island, and the usual complement of aging women in evening dresses with system books at their corrugated elbows (one of them in a wheelchair with a following of young men in black tie standing solemnly behind her watching her betting as if she was performing some kind of numismatic mass).

Shill sat a blackjack table not far from the entrance looking as if she had been born there: féerique and beautiful in a lacy white see-through dress, white boots. She saw us and without the slightest sign of reaction scratched the table for a bit, then folded her hand. It was then that I noticed, behind the big Negro dealer who collected her bet, Warren, standing with another man and watching us with a smoldering half-smile. The man with him was a deeply tanned heavy individual whose frozen physiognomy and seal-sleek tailoring suggested Mafia middle management. Adrian signaled to him and the two men passed between the tables and disappeared behind a curtained door marked PRIVE.

I couldn't tell whether Aunt Lavinia had recognized either Shill or Warren from our near-encounter at the San Francisco airport; she seemed to see them and look momentarily quizzical. Then Lord Bobby—who had naturally not missed anything—proposed they go directly to the private game rooms "to see if they can give us a show." Aunt Lavinia, her attention diverted, agreed. Mrs. Quigley preferred to stay in the main room and play just for fun. As our party was dividing, I saw Shill pick up her chips, pass a couple to the dealer, slip off her chair and without a glance back leave by the curtained door Warren had just closed.

In the next hour at the blackjack table, using a notoriously unsporting system which almost always wins for me (you stand on any combination, including twelve, whenever it can be broken by a hit), I lost $42, or approximately an eighth of my net worth at the time. I watched the door, but neither Warren nor Shill reappeared. When our foursome rejoined at the bar off the main game room, I found that Mrs. Quigley had won seven dollars at roulette; Lord Bobby meanwhile had dropped more than nine hundred at baccarat, while at the same game, Aunt Lavinia, following a brilliant series of bancos, came away with chips worth a little more than eight thousand dollars. So the wheel of fortune turns. As we toasted her good luck, I noticed a familiar face. Standing to one side of the entrance to the bar, wearing a black suit and the regulation dark glasses popular on the island: the voodoo drummer. True to form, Lord Bobby caught my glance, but before he could turn around, the wall-walking percussionist had moved out of sight. I looked at my watch—10:40—wondering whether Shill would keep our late date at the pool. Also whether I should heed Shag's warning and not show up myself. A very strong instinct was telling me to abandon caution, take the bold step, and be at the pool. Very strong. But as Lord Bobby and I waited for the ladies to cash their chips, I had to ask myself: what instinct?

A

NIGHT DIP

---

337. WATER.—*N.* water; serum, serosity; lymph; rheum; diluent.

dilution, maceration, lotion; washing &c. *v.*; im-, mersion; humectation, infiltration, spargefaction, affusion, irrigation, *douche,* balneation, bath.

V. be -watery &c. *adj.*; reek.

add water, water, wet; moisten &c. 339; dilute, dip, immerse; merge; im-, sub-merge; plunge, souse, duck, drown; soak, steep, macerate, pickle, wash, sprinkle, lave, bathe, affuse, splash, swash, douse, drench; dabble, slop, slobber, irrigate, inundate, deluge; syringe, inject, gargle.

The water was rocking but I didn't see her at first; I called, then heard a sudden swirl and a splash in the dark end of the pool and she swam out into the moonlight.

"I always come here to wash the Casino off," she said. "Come on in, Mr. Frog."

Irritably, I told her I didn't have my bathing suit— alarmed that she seemed to have forgotten her promise to help me get the Contract. "Anyway, shouldn't we be—"

"But I don't either," she said and, by way of demonstration, swam a couple of strokes and slowly dove —reappearing seconds later at the poolside near my feet. The night shift of birds was on; the drums were different too—more regular and, it seemed to me, closer.

"And what if someone should happen by?" I asked her, intrigued. She pushed back and drifted into the center of the pool.

"Nobody will, and even if they did, it's Blackout. Blackout always lasts at least an hour at this time of night."

I hesitated. I had decided, over Shag's warning, to trust Shill tonight, and here she was floating around stark naked in a moon-streaked swimming pool and inviting me to keep her company, while Aunt Lavinia was somewhere out in Saint Sebastian, perhaps in danger. But, I told myself, only Shill could lead me to the Contract.

I found a towel in the pitch-black dressing room. At least, I thought, the obscene little red-feathered boy would be home in bed somewhere. Over the drums, distant machine-gun fire paced my steps to the pool. I dove in.

I approached Shill's silhouette.

"You seem at home in the watery element," I said. She disappeared. Seconds later, I felt her hands on my knees and she surfaced near me and said:

"It's my favorite."

"Let's see," I said, "there's Water, Earth, Fire—" For the moment, I couldn't think of the other. I reached for her, but where she had just been there were only great air bubbles percolating to the surface. I dove after her blindly and caught her but she slipped away and swam to the shallow end.

Her hair smelled strongly of chlorine and Breck and there was a sort of deliberateness in that first embrace, an exploration, a sensation excitingly unlike "falling in love"; for indeed we were, then, playing a strange and possibly deadly game with no promise of anything; but then suddenly Shill's legs had somehow floated around

me and our embrace became very undeliberate and un-
gentle. From being a girl of riddles, she was all at once
tremulously communicative, and just for an instant I
sensed she was trying to reach me in some reckless im-
perative way . . .

At this juncture, however, we tumbled over in the
water. Shill was laughing. I remember I swallowed half
the pool. Then I was trying to find the bottom (I had
momentarily lost the sense of where up was) and Shill
caught me in a violent hammer lock and held me down. I
was almost out of breath, choking, water was up my nose,
and I started to struggle but she was strong, and when she
did loosen her hold it was only in order to shove me
deeper in the water, pressing violently on my back, until
I felt her legs now closing around my neck in a "scissors"
grip and then an astounding idea loomed in my oxygen-
starved brain: Shill was not playing voluptuous games at
all—she was trying to kill me!

It is possible that this "realization" saved my life, because with a final desperate effort I freed myself and shot
to the surface, flailing and gasping for breath—air! I had
never heard Shill laughing with genuine amusement before. And—incredibly—she splashed me.

"That ought to teach you, *smartie!*" she said.

Well, I started to reply with hot indignation but she
just kicked up and was out there floating on her back so
that she couldn't hear me. I coughed, watching her rue-
fully. My towel was floating around somewhere on the
bottom of the pool.

No, I thought then: Shill couldn't really have been trying to drown me; for one thing, only a very skilled actress could have counterfeited amusement when I came thrashing out of the water—had she been lethally bent an instant before. The moon entered an archipelago of clouds; the drums, as if responding, hesitated, then picked up again; the birds screeched. Shill must have heard me swimming, breast-stroke, toward her because when I was a couple of yards away she righted herself in the water, and just as I reached for her said:

"Did I tell you I once played Ophelia at the University of Michigan?"

At this, I instinctively became the "murderer" in our aquatic joust (I felt somehow that the manager was watching us from some blacked-out cupola in the hotel) and very soon Shill's writhing evasions, laughter, the night scents, and chance mementos of our other, near-fatal embrace filled me with such a desire to "win" that Shill, impressed, stopped struggling.

"Not here," she whispered in my ear, then bit it.

"Where?" I said.

"Warren's house." My danger-warning system went on again.

"Why Warren's house?"

"Because he isn't there."

"Where is he?" I asked, trying to think.

"It's Tuesday," she explained, still whispering into my wounded ear. "Every Tuesday he has dinner with President Hermoso at the palace. At midnight, because the president is a night person. They sit around and talk till all hours, so the only person at Warren's house is the zombie. That is," she added with a little giggle, "if you want to call him a person."

After this declaration, I was even more doubtful. It is, of course, a notorious fact that a woman, at the very moment she seems most desirable and obtainable, will often slip behind a sort of verbal Chinese screen and start chattering compulsively about zombies or something; however, just then I sensed that it was more than that with Shill: I felt her trembling and suddenly had the distinct impression that the whole evening was supposed to follow a certain scenario of hers—with a definite, predetermined finale.

"What zombie?"

"Ozo."

"Is Ozo a real zombie?"

Shill eased out of my relaxed embrace and leaned against the side of the pool. "Just about as real as they come," she said. "But don't worry, Ozo's harmless as a lamb. Don't tell me you're afraid?"

I asked where the house was and Shill explained that it was about ten minutes out of Saint Sebastian. "Near the water." We could go in her car.

"And there's another thing," she added. "There's something there you might be looking for."

I waited.

"A certain little paper," she said.

"There?"

"Sometimes."

Again, I thought of the warnings in Shag's letter. I remembered that Shill had lied when she told me Timberline was in danger, and I knew that even now she was in some terrible way under Warren's control, even now as I was talking to her. I would be mad to go with her. And yet— Shill seemed to read my thoughts then, for she reached out and put her finger to my lips, then ran it lightly down over my chin, neck, thorax, and under water to the middle of my stomach and pushed.

"Trust me, Mr. Frog," she said.

AT WARREN'S

3. *Contingent Subservience.*

665. DANGER.—*N.* danger, peril, insecurity, jeopardy, risk, hazard, venture, precariousness, slipperiness; instability &c. 149; defencelessness &c. *adj.*

[Dangerous course] leap in the dark &c. (*rashness*) 863; road to ruin, *facilis descensus Averni,* hair-breadth escape.

cause for alarm; source of danger &c. 667. [Approach of danger] rock –, breakers- ahead; storm brewing: clouds -in the horizon, – gathering; warning &c. 668; alarm &c. 669. [Sense of danger] apprehension &c. 860.

hang by a thread, totter; sleep –, stand- on a volcano; sit on a barrel of gunpowder, live in a glass house.

bring –, place –, put- in -danger &c. *n.*; endanger, expose to danger, imperil; jeopard, -ize; compromise; sail too near the wind &c. (*rash*) 863.

HILL drove fast, too fast for the gravel streets that even at midnight were full of people the headlights picked up. The top was down, the moon roved behind the clouds, there was an odor of cooked vegetables and acrid fires in the hot wind that dried our hair. Out of town, the road became a straightaway tunneling through a jungle, came out at a white-sand beach, climbed, then dropped again following the tortuous coast line. We didn't talk. Shill's hair was whipping her face as her long fingers put the car into delicately controlled skids on the inside hairpin turns. She had put on a short blue wrap-around dress at the pool (stowing her dress in a Lufthausa flight bag) and damp spots showed above her breasts; she was driving barefoot. I settled back in the bucket seat and watched the clouds, the moon and the Big Dipper wheeling on the rock-spitting turns.

A squat, ugly stone castle in miniature, built on an isolated rock promontory, with a crenelated donjon and a fat tower squeezed together by thick stone walls—this was Warren's pied-à-terre in the Caribbean. We turned off on a narrow road marked only

DEFENSE D'ENTRER

and approached an arched entrance in the morose walls and halted before a portcullis in the down position. Shill touched a button on the dashboard. There was a whir of machinery and the portcullis started up.

"Very suburban," I said, as we drove under the still-rising iron bars and into the small courtyard. "Where does the electricity come from?"

"Generator," said Shill, pulling up before the massive oak door of the crenelated main building. "The Navy's best." Behind us, the portcullis jangled shut. "Warren has to have the best," she added.

Ahead of us inside the court was a stone hut built against the high wall with a single window in which a dim glaucous light wavered on four dirty panes of glass. I asked who lived there.

"Ozo," she told me.

"Saying his prayers?"

"Don't worry," she said. "Ozo doesn't do anything on his own accord."

On this reassuring note, we got out of the car just as about a hundred tons of Caribbean hit the rocks below us.

"At least," I said, "I hope he has a radio and Thursday nights."

Shill was tense as we entered Warren's grim hide-away; in fact, as she turned on the lights, she was looking at me in a decidedly odd way, searchingly, I might almost say —huntingly. A moment later, however, she became again the surface-assured, brittle, locked-up girl I had first met at the San Francisco airport, and as she turned into the room, she said with an ironical wave, "Home."

Her voice sounded hollowly in the great barren hall-like room where we were standing, with vast expanses of stone floor, high walls, Gothic windows and, for furnishings, little but packing crates like the ones we had seen at Warren's aunt's house. She started across to a low door in the wall opposite the entrance.

"What's all this stuff?" I asked.

"Surplus," she told me. "Watch your head."

She found a light switch and I followed her through the low doorway into the room beyond. When I straightened up, I could hardly believe what I saw.

We were in a fairly small room with a vaulted ceiling, a single small barred window in the left wall, and on the right another small doorway leading to a winding staircase, ascending. The surprising thing was that I had seen this room before. Or one very like it. I recognized the clutter of papers and objects on the desk dramatically spotlighted from above, the table behind the desk with tape recorders, a film projector, strobe lights, the German officer's helmet in the shelves along the wall, the familiar silver trophy, the stuffed quail, the photographs, the shrunken head, the pennant.

It was Warren's old room at school!

Only the roaring of the sea below the window and the high vaulted ceiling and stone walls told me we had not stepped back thirteen years and a few thousand miles to our weird alma mater on the desert.

"Sanctum sanctorum," said Shill, as I went over to examine the photographs in standing mounts on the shelves.

"It's like his room at school," I said. "The same junk."

"He's always talking about that place," she said in a sullen voice, sitting down on a small upholstered prie-dieu. She tossed her head to indicate the door to the stairway. "That goes to the tower room," she added.

"What goes on up there?"

"The bedroom."

"Oh. And who's this?" I had taken down a mounted photograph, crudely hand-colored, of the fierce-looking old woman in the voodoo troupe.

"Mama Céline," Shill explained, glancing, then studying her fingernail and biting it. "She made him a houngan."

"A voodoo priest?"

"Yes. So now he keeps her around like an old nanny."

"What's all this?" I shuffled through the papers on the desk.

"People's little mistakes," she said.

I picked up a letter and started to read:

> Dear Senator Rasmussen,
> Congratulations on your son Clark's forthcoming marriage to Miss Cynthia Van Sickle. What a pity if this joyous occasion should be spoiled by certain revelations of Warrant Officer Bronsalaw Durstin, the washroom attendant at the Princeton Club and Mr. F.C.—

"Good God!" I said. "I suppose the Contract's somewhere here with all this stuff?"

She didn't answer for a moment, then, "It's some-where—" I was about to answer when another letter caught my eye. It was on blue paper with a strange device as the letterhead:

The message was short. It said:

Not another penny!
Baxter

"Who's Baxter?" I said, holding up the blue letter.
"Dr. Baxter."
"Who's he?"
"Well, he's an Englishman, for one thing."
"And for another?"
"He's dead."
I looked up at her.
"Boat accident," she went on, "—officially. The government here is very nice about some things."
She seemed amused by my surprise, then with a slight smile she got up and, trailing her hand along the rough wall, went around to the shelves behind the desk, reached

up and took down the shrunken head and underhanded it to me.

"Catch," she said.

I caught the revolting object and set it on the desk.

"Shill!" I said, thinking of Shag's warning.

She pouted and said, "What happens to me?"

"You obviously ought to leave this island," I said, continuing to search through the papers on the desk. "Why do you stay with him?"

"You mean, a nice girl like me?" Hard. Ironic. Then before I knew what she was doing, she walked over to the table of electronic equipment and suddenly the room went dark. Then it started throbbing with a deep drumming, a low vaguely anthropoid babble; then it was no longer a room but a throbbing, gyrating assault of light patterns—the same audio-visual nightmare I had experienced at the Hawk Club!

"Shill! Shut that off!"

She didn't move. She just stood there fragmented by the pulsing light like a wax figure in a thunderstorm. After a couple of false tries, I stopped the infernal son-et-lumière: mumbling ape voices, drums, lights; and in the darkness we heard the sea pounding on the rocks again.

"Listen," I said, finding the light switch. "He's got you hypnotized and probably drugged, too. Tell me where the Contract is and we'll get you out of here and off the island. You do want to go back to Michigan, don't you?" She watched my now-desperate searching of the desk and the shelves with a twist of amusement on her lips.

"You're not even warm," she said quietly.

I started for another part of the shelves. "Now?"

216

"Colder."

"Over here?"

"Ice cold."

I started back along the shelves.

"A little warmer."

Back to the desk.

"Warmer."

I came around the other side of the desk, nearer Shill.

"Much warmer."

Experimentally, I started toward her.

"Hot," she said.

I took another couple of steps.

"You're getting very hot."

She undid her dress. A little folded piece of ruled paper fluttered down between her breasts.

Neither of us picked it up.

"Mr. Frog," she said, looking up at me as we climbed the stairs, hands locked together. Suddenly, I understood.

"Miss Sleeping Beauty," I answered.

Her hand became like steel.

As we were climbing the stone spiral, I suddenly, for some reason, found myself thinking back to Monique in Paris. She had had a little room in the garret of a dark mediaeval building off the rue de la Huchette. The entrance was in a sunless alley too narrow for anything but a Vespa or a bicycle, a place full of cats going nowhere and an authentic gas lamp that sputtered feeble yellow light on the perpetually damp cobblestones. It was opposite an Arab cafe and next door to a pipe-tapping establishment, with racks of iron and copper tubes visible through a grimy window. One climbed seven flights behind Monique, waited as she fitted the key in the lock, and entered a tiny room almost entirely occupied by a great brass bed . . .

We kissed, standing there in the middle of the circular room with wavering moonlight on the walls and sea-sounds pouring in the open windows; then she said:

"My name isn't Shill. It's Sally. Sally Wood. Shill was his invention. Funny, I haven't even thought about Sally Wood for a long time and now I'm even beginning to feel like her again!" She was suddenly talking in a great rush, kissing me now and then like a drunk taking nips for courage. "I used to hate that name. At Michigan, it was always Sally Would and Sally Wouldn't—everyone was so immature then and I used to feel a thousand years old. I wanted to go to India to the Himalayas and sit at the feet of some old guru and learn something. Part of me wanted that very badly."

"And the other part wanted monsters."

She smiled, suddenly seeming to change into Shill again: a hard smile, To Let signs in her eyes.

"Yes," she said.

"So you joined the C.I.A. in spite of the fact it's very difficult for a girl to do so, and then you met Warren."

"Yes. Substantially, that's it." Then: "Avery, I think I can leave him now." She was Sally again.

"Of course you can," I said. "You could all along except, one way or another, he's had you thinking he had some power over you."

"Well, he has, damn it. And look who's talking. He's got power over quite a few people. Your friend, for instance—"

She had raised her voice to make herself heard over a long tumbling of water under the windows, but when the water stopped tumbling, we both heard the tight snarl of a sport car fading in and out as it approached on the coast road.

"Warren?" I said.

"He's early."

I asked Sally if there was a back way out of the house; she said there was—jammed shut with crates.

"We'll have to stay out of sight in the hall, then get to the car when he's gone into the chapel."

"The chapel?"

"His study."

We ran down to the "chapel"; I found the Contract on the floor and stuffed it into my jacket pocket. Outside there was an electric whir, a steady clanking.

"I forgot the portcullis," she said in a loud whisper.

We waited, our two hearts hammering as one, behind the packing crate nearest the door. The door opened. Warren's steps across the stone floor resounded like shots. The door slammed shut.

"SHILL!" he shouted.

When the light came on in the chapel, we crossed to the door and, by timing our moves to the sea-crashes, got outside into the court. The light in the oleaginous window of the hut wavered cosily.

In the Triumph, Sally looked at me once, then determinedly pressed both the starter button and the button that raised the portcullis. The engine turned over nicely, the portcullis started up.

"OZO!" called a great voice above us.

But the engine wasn't catching.

"Count ten," I suggested.

"OZO!!"

"—four, five, six—" A shadow hulked across the hut window, the portcullis was now almost all the way up.

"ARRETE LO!" shouted Warren from the tower window. "ARRETE VOITURE!"

The door of the hut opened, slipped on its hinges; a wedge of light knifed toward us on the cobbles. A startlingly tall man stood in the doorway, his fuzzy hair fringed with smoky gold light; he stood there a moment, then lurched forward, canting slightly, as if his left leg was asleep, but definitely homing on us.

"—ten." Sally stabbed at the button and the engine caught and started. I could hear, over the sound of waves, Warren shouting in Creole to the zombie; then the towering Negro was close enough so that I caught a glimpse of his face. His hand was on the door on Sally's side when she shot away and out the courtyard in a squeal of tires on the damp cobbles.

"Ozo looked disappointed," I said, as we brodied into the first turn.

"You would too if you thought you were dead," said

Sally, as we came out of the turn inches from the cliff wall and took off into the seaside curve almost broadside. I suggested we slow down and live.

"Warren'll be on us and that 911S of his is a lot faster than this," she explained. I looked back: on the outboard turns, I saw slaloming headlights. I asked where we were going.

"The Rock," she said. "If we can get where there're a lot of tourists around, Warren won't try anything—not right away. Incidentally, there's a gun in the glove compartment."

"That's good."

"Aren't you going to take it? Warren's got an arsenal in that car."

"The last time I had a gun in my hand," I reflected, "I almost killed Mrs. Peabody."

A large Japanese-print wave, caught in the headlights, curled up toward the Triumph, crashed in the darkness behind us. Sally only shrugged slightly. Then as we turned inland and entered the jungle road, she wound the little Triumph up to 70 and the needle was still climbing when we saw the lights ahead. At first I thought they were the outskirts of Porte Sebastian but Sally knew better.

"Road block," she said. "Boom-booms." I glanced back: Warren's lights were already in the straightaway. "End of the tunnel of love," Sally added, downshifting, only it wasn't Sally Wood any more but the hard ironical voice of Shill—I opened the glove compartment and reached for the gun.

"No," she said, stopping my hand. "They'd just mess you up. Let him have his little show. It's best."

"What about you?"

"Me?" she smiled, shrugged again with a still-born laugh. "I guess the University of Michigan will just have to wait a little more."

"The police won't let him take you, will they?"

She laughed out loud and said, "You just watch."

Two jeep station wagons were parked across the road with roof spotlights training on us as Sally braked to a stop on the side of the road. There was a sound of laughter from one of the jeeps, unnatural, clowning laughter. Then silence. After a moment, two silhouettes separated from the glare and started slowly toward us. The spotlight on the jeep nearest us suddenly swung away and illuminated another man on the side of the road opposite us, urinating. There was a new roar of harsh laughter from the first jeep, an order from the second; after another moment, the light swung back on us.

"Pigs!" said Sally—just as Warren's headlights turned the two silhouettes into very convincing representatives of President Hermoso's constabulary.

One carried a sub-machine-gun lazily locked in his arm like a putter, the other's dark glasses were shattered in one lens, eerily spider-webbed by Warren's lights. They stopped in the middle of the road and took up a station there. The Porsche door snapped open. The man who had been urinating got into the first jeep and slammed the door a couple of times, and immediatly there was a sound of violent scuffling, grunts, heavy bodies pounding car metal, mad laughter, cries of mock (?) pain, then the same placid, authoritative voice from the second vehicle. The scuffling subsided. Then, mischievously, the spot-light beam strayed up the road and picked up Warren standing by the door of the Porsche.

"Bonnefoi!" he shouted. "Tell your monkeys to get that light off me!"

More muffled giggling—the light stayed on him.

"BONNEFOI!"

A quiet order from the second jeep and the light swung back on us. I got out of the car, infuriated, and started toward the second jeep to demand that we be allowed to pass; the Boom-boom with the spider-web eyeglasses stepped in front of me, blocking my way. This aroused new idiot laughter. Meanwhile, Sally had gotten out of the car too and stood there in the lights, biting her fingernail, not nervously but abstractedly, as if she was alone in a room.

"Come here, Shill," said Warren quietly.

"Wait a minute, Warren!" I said, starting over to him, only to be blocked now by the man with the machine-gun.

"You forgot the rules, Shill," Warren went on. "No visitors—remember? Come over here."

"Don't, Sally!" I said.

She shrugged listlessly, still biting her nail, as if the pro-ceedings didn't directly concern her.

"Warren!" I said, trying to get past the Boom-boom. "She doesn't want to go with you!" Then I turned to the glare of the jeeps' lights and was about to protest to the invisible "authority," but my intention was anticipated

223

and greeted with still more demented laughter, in which this time I felt even the "authority" joined.

"Sorry," said Warren, "but as you see, the concept of private property still means something on this island. What is it they say?—a man's home is his castle? It is rather like a castle, isn't it? Small, though, didn't you think? There's a wreck in the water—you can see the bridge awash in the daytime. Greek cruise ship, Panamanian registry. They say it went down with the full orchestra playing. They say sometimes you can still hear the tune. Come over here." The order was for Sally. She stood there a moment, indifferent to the lights, then started over to Warren. There was a round of ironical applause and metallic thumping from the first jeep.

"What about Michigan, Sally?" I called to her, astonished by her sudden obedience to Warren's commands.

"One of her pipe dreams," he answered for her. "We all have them. But you can't turn back the past, can you, Avery? Give me the Contract."

I couldn't believe it. Had Warren in the minute or two he had been in the house made the discovery that the Contract had been taken?

"I don't have it," I lied.

"No? How about it, Shill?"

As she came toward me, I was too surprised to move. I didn't even object when she opened my jacket, took out the Contract and playfully fanned my nose with it.

The Boom-booms drove me back to the hotel. I sat up front in the second jeep. The two men who had gotten out and stood in the road were in the back seat apparently trying to commit gross indecencies on one another, for their knees kept ramming my seat and driving me forward. The driver—the voice of authority—paid no attention to them but spent the few minutes of our ride glancing away from the road, grinning genially at me and, in studied but unpracticed English, inquiring after my impressions of Saint Sebastian. He was a man of about forty, with an affability incubated, no doubt, around cockpits and police-station cellars; small calculating eyes, a gold front tooth; and even through the boiling outrage I felt at that moment, I sensed that, for all the absurd banalities we exchanged, my conductor already saw the two of us allied in some rank and dubious fashion.

MORE

CONTACTS

---

248. [Complex circularity.]—CON-
VOLUTION.—*N.* winding &c. *v.*; con-,
in-, circum-volution; wave, undula-
tion, tortuosity, anfractuosity; sinu-
osity, -ation; meandering, circuit,
circumbendibus, twist, twirl, windings
and turnings, *ambages;* torsion; inos-
culation; reticulation &c. (*crossing*)
219.

involved, intricate, complicated,
perplexed; labyrinth-ic, -ian, -ine; per-
istaltic; dædalian.

Adv. in and out, round and round.

HE next morning over breakfast, I suggested to Aunt Lavinia that we leave the island that same afternoon, proposing Aruba (where she had acquaintances staying at the Palm Beach Club) as an intermediate stop before our return to San Francisco. We could scarcely hear each other for the birds chirruping all around the terrace. When she had understood me, my aunt looked surprised.

"But why, Avery?"

"Political trouble," I told her. "It's safer in Aruba."

"Political trouble? Here? Where did you hear that? Lord Bobby didn't say anything about any political trouble. As a matter of fact," she added, after a moment's thought, "he's taking us out on a glass-bottom boat this afternoon." I neglected to mention that Aunt Lavinia was wearing a straw hat that morning with a single spire in the center which made it resemble a Siamese temple. "And we have reservations for three more days. And our tickets. And there's the voodoo show tonight. Besides," she concluded unexpectedly, "I'm quite surprised you would want to leave with that girl who's come all this way."

"What girl?" I asked cautiously, wondering at that instant how Aunt Lavinia could have found out about Sally.

"What girl! Don't be silly. The one Freddie brought. The one you seemed to know. Timbermine, or whatever her name is. Didn't she find you last night?"

"No," I said.

Hiding my surprise, I learned that Timberline had arrived on the evening plane and must have reached the hotel only moments after we had all left for the Casino. With a pang, I realized that she must have been waiting for me alone at the hotel during my whole encounter with Sally.

Then it struck me: Timberline was the "reinforcements" Mrs. Peabody had promised!

"I've already asked her to join our table," my aunt was saying, adding in a rare display of humor, "I think that should settle the political trouble, shouldn't it?"

Ozo gave me a bad scare. I was walking fast through the gardens in the direction of the pool, hoping to find Timberline there, when he stepped from behind a royal palm and stood there in the middle of the path not six feet from me, slightly out of plumb.

"Ozo," I said. "What are you doing here?"

I could have been talking to a cigar-store Indian. Then I saw that he had a piece of paper in his hand.

"Is that a note for me, Ozo? From Mr. Oliphant?"

He didn't move. With the din of birds and the filtered sunlight wavering on the zombie, the scene was rather peculiar. Then he cleared his throat with a sort of rattle, as if he was unaccustomed to speaking.

"Mauvais," he said at last.

"What's mauvais, Ozo? Is Mr. Oliphant mauvais?"

"Oui. Mauvais."

"Yes, I agree. Now, is that—Est-ce que ça c'est un message pour moi?"

"Oui."

"Alors," I said.

But he made no move to deliver the note. After a moment, he said something I couldn't understand. I asked him to repeat it. He did. "You say you have a cousin in Miami?" I said.

"Oui."

"Well, what about it? How does that concern me? En quoi est-ce que—"

"You—sponsor?"

"Sponsor?"

"Sponsor," he confirmed, "so Ozo go to the United States. Saint Sebastian no good. Mauvais. Bad country."

"But I'm afraid I can't do that, Ozo. I'm sorry, but—"

"Miss Shill say you sponsor Ozo," he said reproachfully and quite clearly.

"She said that?"

"Oui."

"Well, she shouldn't have," I told him firmly. "She had no right to say that." I looked again at the note he held. "Is that note from Miss Shill?"

"Oui. She say—important."

231

"Well, then—give it to me," I said, in a tone of authority. "Just give it here, Ozo."

"You sponsor?"

"No," I said.

"Very bad for Ozo here. Mr. Oliphant will be very hangry." I had a sudden inspiration.

"What about your cousin in Miami? Why can't he sponsor you?"

"Cousin have no money. Must have money to sponsor."

"Ah," I said, "I don't have any money, either. So I can't sponsor you either. So give me that note." I advanced a step but Ozo put the envelope behind him.

"Mr. Oliphant say tomorrow you have much money."

"Mr. Oliphant said that?" I could hear laughter from the pool. Splashes. "What else did he say?"

"He say to Miss Shill she must not see you no more. He very hangry. He say Miss Shill unloyal to him. Ungrateful, he say. They fight. After Mr. Oliphant goes to Casino, she tells me I must not stay with Mr. Oliphant. She say I don't have to obey him no more and you sponsor. Then she gives me this note. You sponsor? You—"

Ozo stopped in mid-sentence, his eyes widened, he was looking just past my shoulder. I turned and saw only a thicket of bougainvillea, until I made out in the intricate tapestry of foliage, tendrils and luscious pink blossoms the countenance of the police captain Bonnefoi, gold tooth and all. Ozo let out a cry and ran down the path, then cut into the gardens in the direction of the road, leaving a wake of startled birds, whose raucous warning calls, however, subsided almost immediately. Bonnefoi stepped grandly out of the shrubbery, watching Ozo's sudden departure with a look of philosophical amusement. Then we were both staring at the envelope which had fluttered to the ground midway between us.

"Even the zombies want to go to America," he said, still looking abstractedly at the envelope.

"Land of opportunity," I said, wondering if Bonnefoi would object if I picked it up.

"For some," he said with an auriferous grin, "but for others, Saint Sebastian is the—as you say—land of opportunity. Your friend last night, for instance."

"Warren's no friend of mine," I said. "We just happened to know each other once."

"Perhaps," said the policeman, his eyes floating like fish in his dark glasses, "I should say business acquaintances?"

I grinned back at him and asked him where he got his good English. Obviously pleased, he said the Calvert School and asked if I'd heard of it. I told him I had, wondering all the time what Bonnefoi might know about Warren and me and the Contract.

"I have a diploma. You would like to see it?"

"Not particularly, thanks," I told him and, pointing to the envelope on the path, said, "I think that's for me. Do you mind?"

"Of course not," he said, and I picked up Sally's message.

"Education is a most important consideration in our country," he went on; "for example, our present Foreign Minister has practically none at all."

233

"I think you should be Foreign Minister," I said jocularly on a sudden hunch. Immediately, Bonnefoi's face assumed a deep parliamentary gravity, then broke into another broad, golden grin.

"I like you," he said. "Come, I take you to a nice place where we talk and have a drink."

I thought of continuing in search of Timberline but then made a sudden decision to explore further into Saint Sebastian politics.

On the jolting ride through Porte Sebastian's alluvial streets, I read Shill's note.

> Dear Avery,
>
> Keep your aunt away from the voodoo show tonight! I don't know exactly what is supposed to happen but he had the drummer in the chapel for an hour this morning and that always means the same thing. Trust me *this time* because I am fighting the battle of my life.
> Your
>
> > Sally
>
> P.S. I had to tell Ozo you might sponsor his entry to the U.S. so he would bring you this. He has a cousin or something in Miami.

AT
MAMA TIA'S

seraglio, harem; brothel, bagnio, stew, bawdy-house, *lupanar,* house of ill fame, *bordel.*

B<small>ONNEFOI'S</small> "nice place" turned out to be the leading, in fact the only, interracial brothel in Porte Sebastian, which is called The Pelican Club but better known throughout the Caribbean sporting world as Mama Tia's. You come to it on the north shore road opposite an Esso station, where a faded orange-and-brown sign announces, under the name:

WELCOME TO DRINK, LUNCH DINE AND DANCE
IN AIR CONDITIONED. OPEN 24 HOURS
FLOOR SHOW, SWIMMING POOL, MAGIC

There is a real person named Mama Tia who skippers the establishment, but Bonnefoi, I learned, enjoys certain territorial rights here and delivers the monthly pay-off to the palace treasury and also serves on demand as Mama Tia's sexual partner. As far as I could find out, Bonnefoi had no other home but The Pelican Club and the police station, and I observed a change come over him as we

237

entered the low, ochreous building fronting on the road that housed the public entertainment facilities. He became at once both proprietary and giddy, like a servant showing off his master's house, and it suddenly struck me that Bonnefoi suffered, second by second, from an acute and chronic sense of insecurity.

"The air-conditioning doesn't work at the present time," he announced, with a sweeping gesture that took in a glowering juke box of another day, a long bar, a Red Cap Ale sign with bubbles motionless in dark tubes, a faded picture of Joe Louis, a larger framed photograph of President Hermoso hanging over the cash register, and the mute air-conditioner straddling the window.

"Plenty of action here every night," he said, as we passed on through the vacant bar and down three worn steps and into a spacious palm-shaded compound of buildings. My guide pointed out Mama Tia's own tidy-looking house and headquarters, the staff's lodgings, a laundry and, farther back, the dozen or so small cabins where the girls received. (Some, Bonnefoi assured me, were as young as thirteen and very nice.) Throughout the compound there was a note of order and almost Helvetian efficiency about the place: a woman was distributing clean towels to the cabins, a stocky young man with an anthracite complexion was feeding chickens, while near his head two small red, white and blue simians in a large cage hanging from a tree licked themselves. Orchids flowered in the crotches and burls of the trees and a neatly tended bed of birds of paradise grew near a cinder-block wall. Even the ornithological life here was less strident and more musical than at Paradise Roc.

238

Behind her screen door I beheld, vaguely, the great mahogany head of Mama Tia.

"Mama Tia! I have come with a friend!" said Bonnefoi with inflated enthusiasm.

The screen door stayed shut. The head did not move or speak.

"Let us in, Mama. We have come to talk and have a drink. Also," added the police captain, with a craven wink at me, "he says he wants to see my diploma."

"We're cleaning," said the head in perfect English. "You can go to the swimming pool. What is it that you want to drink?"

"White Horse," said Bonnefoi, beaming as if he was relieved that everything was turning out so well. Mama Tia issued a brief order, the anthracite chicken feeder started for the bar, and Bonnefoi marched me off in the direction of the swimming pool as if I was a regiment.

It was a small, crude affair made of wood lined with canvas, fed by a trickle from a plastic pipe, one side of the wooden frame extending as a platform just large enough to accommodate two round metal tables shaded by faded and patched pink umbrellas apparently inherited from Paradise Roc. We sat at one of the tables. The chicken feeder arrived with the White Horse, glasses, a plastic ice bucket and soda and left the lot. Bonnefoi poured me a stiff one and the same for himself. He raised his glass, looked thoughtfully at it a moment, then at me, smiled and drank off half of it.

"If you have enough money, you can have a virgin,"

he said with a wave in the direction of the cabins. "If you have enough money, you can have anything." He looked at his glass again and added, "Some day perhaps I will go to America." The captain had fixed me with a speculative look, seeming to make no connection between this remark and his recent disparagement of the zombie's desire to emigrate. Then he asked me how I liked Saint Sebastian. I told him fine. Bonnefoi then scratched his genitals abstractedly, as if he was considering something. Then he asked me if I'd ever heard of him in America. I told him I hadn't but that I'd heard about the Boombooms.

"What did you hear?" he wanted to know.

"Oh, just that your boys are pretty efficient and don't mind working late hours. Things like that." He beamed—then suddenly looked grim.

"Your friend has done very well here," he said, laying his huge hand on the head of a black dog that had come up on the platform and rested his chin on his knee. "He is a very clever man. Very clever. Very friendly with the President. Very clever." It was clear as he reiterated these compliments that they cost him an effort.

"I told you he's no friend of mine," I said, "and no business acquaintance either."

"You find out he won't do business, no?"

"What are you talking about?"

My surprised reaction only seemed to assure him he was on the right track.

"You come here with your aunt. She is very rich lady. Got plenty of money. So you meet with your friend and you ask him to do you a favor. Like you ask a friend to do you a favor. You say to yourself, my friend is very clever and knows the voodoo ways, and he knows how to make it look nice and quiet. But he say to you: no thank you friend."

"But he didn't say no thank you friend!" I told him. "I mean he *is* trying to kill her, but I don't want him to. You've got it backwards. Do you understand? I want you to stop him!"

Bonnefoi looked at me with interest, patting the dog.

"You like his girl," he said shrewdly.

"Look," I said, taking out Shill's letter and handing it to him. "Read that."

Lips moving, he did. Puzzlement clouded his face, then slowly cleared.

"Perhaps, then, you and the girl would like to have Mr. Oliphant—" He clicked his tongue and made a small spiral with his forefinger.

"Perhaps," I said, playing the game. "Wouldn't you?"

"Perhaps—perhaps not. But Jean Bonnefoi does not arrest friends of the President. Very unpatriotic."

At this point, I experienced sudden alarm. The policeman was either refusing to believe that Aunt Lavinia was in peril or didn't care. I tried to convince him that Warren was actually preparing to have her murdered at the voodoo show, but nothing seemed to make an impression until I mentioned the ouanga. That had an immediate effect, and he listened closely as I described the crossed sticks tied with red ribbon and the circumstances in which the thing was found.

"The maid at the Rock will tell you," I finished. "Or ask the manager."

He looked at me a long time and I observed a new sort of animation happening behind his dark glasses.

"He would not be so crazy," he said at last, leaning toward me across the table and bringing his face so close to mine that I could see little pits on his gold tooth.

"Why not?" I asked, noticing my own longish Anglo-Saxon face twinned in his glasses.

Just then we both heard steps mounting the platform and turned to see the coal-black factotum starting to sweep the platform. Bonnefoi was about to say something crisp to him when a sharp call from behind the screen door stopped him and he called back, "Ouais, ouais, Mama Tia," then turned to me and said:

"Come, we go some place else while he sweep. I tell you some things."

Bonnefoi took the scotch, I took the plastic ice bucket and, our glasses in hand, followed by the dog, we crossed the sun-splotched compound, wading through a flock of feeding chickens, and went over to an ancient automobile of European extraction, a Panhard or something, less motor and wheels, and sat down cautiously on the running board. The scotch and ice we put on the hard-packed ground geometrically between us. Bonnefoi extracted a brown cigarette from his tunic, stared at it reproachfully, then lit it and began to talk. Some of it I had already heard, but this was Bonnefoi's personal version of Warren's singular career on Saint Sebastian, a version which though colored by Bonnefoi's jealousy (and God knows what other primitive affections) checked out pretty well with both Shag's Indian friend's account and Sally's. Warren had come to the island five years before as an agent for Eastern interests to work out a gambling concession with the former government. At that time, however, the Hermoso revolution was under way and Warren, who had soon found the island to his liking, aided the effort by supplying obsolete and rejected arms and ammunition. In grateful recognition, the new dictator, once in power, had let Warren set up his black-mail and cash-and-carry murder operations, granted him the casino concession—personally, cutting out the Eastern interests—and, of course, assured him the full co-opera-tion of the police in all these enterprises. Meanwhile, un-known to anyone at first, Warren had become an acolyte in voodoo ceremonies, eventually a houngan, and an adept at some of the more esoteric and forbidden prac-tices of the cult. As Bonnefoi spoke of these dark mat-ters, I watched his face in profile against the background of a whirring chicken that had narrowly escaped skew-ering on a pointed stick he had picked up: it had a de-cidedly savage cast.

However, as he continued (now abstractedly sketch-ing a pair of copulating serpents on the packed ground) I understood that there were other forces at work within the "revolutionary" power structure—notably the Min-ister of Tourism. This man had apparently viewed Warren's activities—particularly his exploitation of se-

lected wealthy tourists—as violations of his own preroga-
tives and, after long brooding about it, had hit on an idea:
he had convinced the President that Warren's operations
were hurting Saint Sebastian's tourist trade, the national
economy and therefore the President's personal income.
Reform was immediate. The President issued an edict.
"So today in Saint Sebastian," Bonnefoi told me, "it is a
crime to harm a tourist—punishable by—" He drew a
slow line across his throat.

He studied my surprised reaction a moment, then went
on scratching at the ground. "Your friend is clever," he
said. "He jump like a rabbit. When the President make
the edict, Oliphant he say oh yes he will obey the law and
he tell him a lot of lies too and—"

"And they're still friends?"

"Yes," said the police captain, evidently with an effort.
"He still very friendly with the President. And now he
obey the law."

"What about the Englishman? Baxter."

I saw I had moved a little too fast for Bonnefoi's liking.

"Dr. Baxter he drown in a boat," he said.

"No he didn't," I said, taking a chance that Sally's information was right. "Why didn't you arrest Oliphant
then?"

"Two reason," said Bonnefoi, after a full minute's silence. "First, I have no proof. Everybody know but nobody say nothing. Dr. Baxter was enemy of your friend,
he talk against him to the President. Second, the—accident happen the day before the edict. Now it is different
and your friend is—"

"I know," I said, "my friend is very clever—but he also has an extremely good reason to kill my aunt—at least he thinks he does—and that's what counts, isn't it?"

"What reason?" asked Bonnefoi, amused at my emotionalism but a little impressed too. "Money?"

"*More* money," I told him, pressing a button on his tunic, "than you ever dreamed of in your whole life. Imagine that!" Then, seeing that he was impressed in earnest now, I added that there was even more to it than money. I reached out and sloshed more White Horse in his glass and mine, sensing suddenly that it was not so much the meaning of what I was saying as the rhetorical effects that held his attention. I noticed that in his absorption he had forgotten about the chickens, which were now foolishly pecking around our feet. I took the stick out of his hand and poked a spotted rooster quite accurately.

"He has a sense of personal insufficiency," I said as we watched the result, "a deep resentment of something, megalomania—who knows what's really behind his obsession. And of course we can't forget the sort of society he comes from, with its stress on violence and material values, can we?"

A smile had unveiled Bonnefoi's gold incisor again. We had rapport. I asked him if he believed at last that Warren was really planning Aunt Lavinia's assassination.

"Maybe he do," he said. "Maybe he is crazy enough."

"Then you'll be at The Rock tonight?"

"Yes, I be there. Don't you worry about nothing. I be there."

But all of a sudden, I *was* worrying. Bonnefoi's look of malicious pleasure was becoming legible.

"Of course, you'll stop him if he tries anything, won't you? You'll—"

"Don't you worry," he said, slapping me on the knee. "Everything going to be all right!" The dog, recognizing the captain's benevolent mood, got up from the ground and came up to him, but Bonnefoi shoved its muzzle aside, reached in his back pocket for his wallet, took it out and after a short search handed me a greasy card. It said simply:

"A toutes heures, a tous prix"

POMPES FUNEBRES

Porte Sebastian   Jean Bonnefoi

"Don't worry," he said again, "everything going to be all right. Everything first-class. You keep the card." Then he got up from the running board and started toward the screen door.

"Hey, Mama Tia!"

Bonnefoi drove me back to the hotel in his police jeep, letting me off at the hotel gates at the foot of the horse-shoe drive. I was still trying to appeal to his sense of duty when he grinned, waved fraternally and dropped in the clutch.

246

LORD BOBBY'S

SECRET

MISSION

714. CONCORD.—*N.* concord, accord, harmony, symphony; agreement &c. 23; sympathy &c. (*love*) 897; response; union, unison, unity; bonds of harmony; peace &c. 721; unanimity &c. (*assent*) 488; league &c. 712; happy family.

Adj. concordant, congenial; agreeing &c. *v.*; in-accord &c. *n.*; harmonious, united, cemented; banded together &c. 712; allied; friendly &c. 888; fraternal; conciliatory; at one with; of one mind &c. (*assent*) 488.

PEOPLE were already at lunch on the terrace and though by now I was definitely feeling the White Horse, I made it, with ballistic accuracy, to our table, where I sat down with my aunt, Mrs. Quigley, Lord Bobby and Timberline.

My reactions upon seeing Timberline again were multiple and unexpected. First, I experienced a sudden seizure of guilt relative to Sally. The worst of it passed quickly, however. Then I noticed how cool and at ease she looked sitting there in the shadow of the pink umbrella. She was wearing a tasteful blue-and-white print sheath, no jewelry, her Montrachet hair sweeping in slow waves past her green eyes, which were just then appraising me coolly but, I decided, not altogether coolly.

"Oh, here's Avery," said Aunt Lavinia. "We were wondering what happened to you."

"Sightseeing," I said, still looking at Timberline. "Hello, Timberline."

249

"Hello," she said, with a faint smile.

"We didn't miss you in the least," said my aunt. "Lord Bobby has been telling us the most fascinating things about voodoo. It's a religion, you know, Avery."

New York, I thought, I'll go with Timberline to New York.

"Fascinating things," agreed Mrs. Quigley. "Makes my skin crawl."

"Rudiments," said Lord Bobby briskly. "You see, they have various god-spirits called loas. There's Damballa, Legba, Papa Zaca—"

Timberline could sculpt and I could finish my play and we would have a little apartment with lots of records and Mexican glass and—

"—Baron Samedi—each with its almost human personality, its own qualities, powers and frailties—"

—creative friends—

"—and like the earliest gods of ancient Greece often intervene in human affairs, summoned by the drums and ritual invocations of the houngans, while the chorus of serviteurs stamps and sways."

"We were in Greece recently," remarked Aunt Lavinia.

—and get away from San Francisco and chocolate winds and Bachelors' Balls and Pat and Gordon and Witter and the Princess and Mrs. Stockbacker and trips with Aunt Lavinia—

"—ritual participation in the invisible world—"

Timberline and I would travel everywhere, wherever fascinating people congregate. Ischia, for example.

—"loa is fetched and actually possesses one or more of

the adepts—makes his modest wishes known through those possessed—"

I would take her free ballooning in Holland.

"—accompanied by the sacrifice of small animals."

"You mean they actually kill animals?" asked Mrs. Quigley.

We would charter a boat and visit all the Greek islands, one after the other—

"—never tell about the so-called voodoo they put on for spectators—mostly corrupted, of course, debased—"

—masked balls in Venice, the film festival in Cannes, Paris, Rome, la dolce vita—

"—can be dangerous."

"Dangerous?" asked Aunt Lavinia. "I don't understand, Lord Bobby."

I was racing along the Riviera in a red Maserati with Timberline beside me when I suddenly came out of it: Aunt Lavinia was staring at Lord Bobby with a look of consternation, Mrs. Quigley was apparently still troubled by the thought of animal sacrifice, Timberline seemed amused by something, and Lord Bobby was looking at me in a way I didn't like. He seemed to be about to reply pointedly to Aunt Lavinia's question but changed his mind and only said, still looking at me:

"Of course, in the end it's all a lot of superstitious nonsense, isn't it?"

The waiter brought coffee. I took out my Kaywoodie and coolly filled and lit it. Mrs. Quigley looked up and said:

"At least I hope there won't be any horrors tonight. I can't stand it when there're horrors."

251

THE CONTRACT

After lunch, Timberline and I strolled through the birdfest in the gardens, found a stone bench opposite a wooden statue of a male figure half-concealed in leaves and sat down. I sensed that Timberline was still very distant.

"Look," I said, "Aunt Lavinia really is in trouble. I had to leave San Francisco that way. I tried to call you but—"

"Avery."

"Yes?"

"Why didn't you tell me?"

"You mean about—"

"Yes. Mrs. Peabody told me everything. Do you realize that wonderful old lady still has confidence in you in spite of everything?"

"But you don't."

"Avery, how could you get involved in such a ridiculous agreement?"

"I don't know. I was a lot younger then and it was very hot. We had had some rum. Also, it seemed funny at the time. And incidentally, I did tell you—at least I tried to tell you but you didn't think I was serious."

"But then why bring her *here*, of all places, where *he* is? Mrs. Peabody said it wasn't your idea but—"

"She's right. It wasn't."

"Avery?"

"What?"

"You'd inherit a lot of money if anything happened to Aunt Lavinia, wouldn't you? I mean, an awful lot."

"Yes."

"I wouldn't have any idea even how much a lot was," she said after a moment.

"Well, for instance, four and a half million is rather a lot."

She traced an arc in the path with the point of her shoe.

"Of course," I added, "that's before taxes."

"Oh, yes, of course—but there's something left, isn't there?"

"Yes. Quite a lot, in fact."

We both sat there looking at the wooden figure across the path.

Then I told her Warren was going to try to kill Aunt Lavinia at the voodoo show. For a long time she looked at me. I said:

"I don't want him to"—and I saw she believed me.

At that instant, I was aware of something moving in the shrubbery behind us. I turned and saw a stirring of red, plunged into the undergrowth—but I wasn't fast enough. By the time I'd found the tunnel-like path in the dense growth, my quarry had disappeared. I came back to Timberline and told her about the little boy who had been following me around. "I don't know what he was doing there," I said, "but you can bet it was for money."

"Avery."

"Yes?"

"Shouldn't we be doing something about your aunt? Like getting her off the island or something?"

"I've been trying," I told her, gratefully noticing the "we," "but she doesn't want to go yet. Partly because of Lord Bobby, I think. Listen, what do you make of Lord Bobby? What was your impression?"

"He seems all right," she said, her mind apparently somewhere else. "Avery."

"Yes."

"How did you find out about—your aunt and to-night?"

"That girl that's with him. The one we saw in San Francisco."

"She just—told you?"

"Yes. You see, she's actually on our side."

"Really?"

"Yes. At least, I think she is. She's back with him now but she got a note to me this morning and— Back at the house," I explained, when I noticed Timberline wasn't reacting much.

"Go on," she said finally. "What's she like, for instance?"

I thought a moment.

"She went to the University of Michigan," I told her cautiously.

"I thought she went to Foxcroft. Did she go to Foxcroft and then the University of Michigan?"

"Yes," I said. "As a matter of fact, after Michigan, she went to the C.I.A."

"When did she tell you all this?"

"Last night, when we were trying to get the Contract back—"

"—at the house. Your friend's house."

"Yes."

"And where was he all this time?"

"Having dinner with the President."

"And?"

"And—we got it back. But then he caught us and got it back again. Now he probably has her drugged and hypnotized and— But she did send the note."

"Mrs. Peabody was right."

"What do you mean?"

"You need all the help you can get." Then she was looking past my shoulder. "Look—here comes Lord Bobby."

He was halfway up the path, carrying a swagger stick, swinging it smartly. As he came up to us he greeted us, apologized for intruding, planted his swagger stick in the path, opened it and sat down facing us with his arms folded expectantly and looked from one to the other of us for several seconds before settling his hawk-like gaze on me.

"In an hour," he began, "I am escorting your aunt and Mrs. Quigley on a glass-bottom boat expedition. Both ladies assure me they share my fascination for the wonders of the deep."

After this overture he beamed, blinked several times, then added that he thought the time had come for us all to put our cards on the table.

"What cards?" I asked warily.

He seemed to detonate internally. I'd never heard a laugh quite like it. "I have a strong feeling," he went on, "that our purposes on this island are—compatible, Mr. Ashley."

"You weren't so sure of that this morning," I told him, thinking suddenly of the "glass-bottom boat expedition" and the ambiguous fate of Dr. Baxter.

"No," he agreed, "I wasn't. But have no fear, Mr. Ashley, I'll present my explanations first." He removed a ring from the little finger of his left hand and passed it to Timberline. It was a plain but massive gold signet ring with a black intaglio. Timberline looked at it and handed it to me. I saw that the intaglio represented a hooded falcon—the same device I had seen on the letter on Warren's desk.

"I doubt," Lord Bobby was saying as I handed the ring back to him, "whether you've heard of the organization that insignia stands for—very unlikely. There are only eleven members—in fact, only ten at the moment because a vacancy exists. We call ourselves the Peregrine Society."

"A falconry club?" I asked.

"Not exactly, Mr. Ashley. Rather difficult, indeed, to describe the exact objectives of our little group. Fact, you might even say we haven't any—at least, not a priori. And that explains the hooded hunter, doesn't it? You see, our principal activity is talk. Quite good talk. First-rate talk, often. Food and wine a secondary consideration. And then at every meeting, some one of us reads a paper.

About anything under the sun—or beyond the sun, for that matter.

"Oh, mostly we stay fairly close to our own areas of activity—part of it is learning each other's languages, you see. Among our members we've had the owner of a large chain of newspapers, a theoretical physicist, a poet, an industrialist or two, an economist, two eminent historians, a doctor, and a very high-ranking member of our government who came to the meetings simply as Mr. Bigelow. And, oh yes, we had a fellow who earned his living tutoring in philosophy at Oxford. Very disappointing. As for me, I represent international banking. Except for wartime, we have met every other Tuesday at a very good restaurant in London for the past thirty years. Of course, a few of the original chaps have passed away, including Mr. Bigelow and the philosopher—"

"And the doctor," I said. "Dr. Baxter."

"Exactly," said Lord Bobby, fixing me with an intense look, but showing no other sign of surprise. "Dr. Baxter."

"Who's Dr. Baxter?" Timberline wanted to know.

"Dr. William Thackery Baxter," said Lord Bobby, still looking at me. "A good friend, a magnificent scientist, a fellow member of the Peregrine Society—now dead." He pivoted and faced Timberline. "You see, my dear, the two of us came to this island years ago on what was then an extremely confidential mission. His Majesty's Service. Remember we weren't sure we were going to win the war then. I, for example, was busy searching parts of the world for safe depositories for securities and currency—if we ever needed them. Dr. Baxter had another mission." Lord Bobby hesitated, then: "We meant to resist if we were occupied—Hitler's thousand years, if necessary—by any and all effective means. Any means—the less predictable and more difficult to detect and combat, the better."

Timberline said, "You mean this Dr. Baxter was here studying—"

"The less said of it all, the better, even today," Lord Bobby interrupted. "However, I can tell you that Baxter's investigations into the lore and pharmacopoeia used on this island were only a small part of his world-wide researches. But they were indeed a part, and unfortunately, it was to this island that Baxter was drawn. He returned here after the war. Learned the patois. Over the years, he came back a number of times, made friends, doctored the natives, stayed longer and longer periods, gained considerable influence in the government Hermoso overthrew—eventually ran afoul of Warren Oliphant.

"I still don't know quite how your friend managed it. It's possible there were things in Baxter's life he was desperately anxious to keep buried, but I think it was something else. I think that Baxter, for all his acquired knowledge of voodoo, was led by his scientific curiosity into some terrible trap set for him by Oliphant, acting out of jealous rivalry (remember, Oliphant is a white houngan)."

Lord Bobby's voice darkened and his tufted brows drew together, then he went on:

"The first sign we had that anything was wrong was

258

when Baxter, a man of large independent means, began drawing greater and greater drafts on his London accounts. Letters stopped. Inquiries went unanswered—until one day, an oddly stilted letter reached me—even the handwriting seemed hardly like Baxter's—saying that he wanted to establish some sort of arts and crafts center here in Porte Sebastian. That was to explain the drafts. The next thing I learned was from Baxter's solicitor—Baxter was dead. Drowned, the government report maintained, lost off a small fishing boat in a storm. The body, they said, was never recovered."

"That wasn't what happened," I suggested.

"So far as anyone knew, Baxter had never fished in his life, and what's more, there was no storm on the day of the alleged drowning—nor that entire week. The story was not even thoughtfully contrived. So—with the full backing and support of the Peregrine Society—I came here at once to investigate the disappearance and if foul play was involved— We have no extradition treaty or diplomatic relations with this singular country, any more than yours does at present."

Lord Bobby was looking at me to see if I'd gotten the point. I had. I asked him how he had gotten on Warren's track.

"I found that toward the end, Baxter had often been to the casino, never to gamble much—he had a loathing of gambling—but he'd sit at a table for a while, then, on a sign from that young lady of Oliphant's, he'd slip into his private office. They were sometimes seen leaving together in his car. I managed to find out that Baxter's funds were credited to Oliphant's personal account here, and subsequently withdrawn in dollars. Of course, no trace of any art center. They say," he added after a hesitation, "that just before he disappeared, Baxter didn't seem to know who he was."

"Oliphant's trying to kill Aunt Lavinia," I told him.

"I know it, dear boy," he said quickly. "I suspected your aunt was in danger the moment I heard they'd put the ouanga in her room. Baxter received an identical one. Trouble was, I didn't know quite how you fitted into the picture. You see, there's an old tradition on this island of cashing wealthy relatives, to put it crudely. Then when I saw you speaking with the girl at the pool— No offense, but you see I couldn't take a chance on your being in league with the man who killed Thack Baxter."

I asked what made him sure I wasn't.

"This," he said, reaching into his blazer pocket and taking out a miniature transistor tape recorder and switching it on.

"—I don't want him to—" I heard my voice say.

He handed me the tape and told me to keep it. I put it in my pocket with Bonnefoi's card and Sally's note.

"The little kid with the feathers?"

"Apologies. But you see I had to be quite sure. Now— are we partners or aren't we?"

I decided to tell Lord Bobby about the Contract and what had happened since Warren's appearance in San Francisco: Aunt Lavinia's narrow escape from the rocket blast, her unlucky decision to come to the island, my visit to Warren's house (and the discovery of Baxter's letter), Sally's warning message and my conversations with Bonnefoi.

"Good Heavens!" said Lord Bobby when I had finished. "Imagine ever letting such a scruffy fellow into a good school." He looked at me a moment, then added: "I say, it all puts you in a rather interesting position, doesn't it, old boy? Why, with four and a half million dollars in the cooky jar, many a chap would—"

"Avery wouldn't," said Timberline, taking my arm.

"Of course not," agreed Lord Bobby. "Though you say Oliphant did reach you once with his system of hypnotism and drugs. Yes, that's his real power; that's what brought Baxter to his ruin. No one today knows the limits of such techniques. I believe Baxter himself was trying to probe the secret of Oliphant's extraordinary gifts when he fell victim to him. Very dangerous. The girl Sally seems to be under his control right now."

"But she did send the note about the drummer," I reminded him.

"Avery thinks she's on our side," put in Timberline.

"Perhaps she is," said Lord Bobby. "In any case, we have to assume the warning is authentic. But what about our friend the police captain? I gather he's hoping that Oliphant's percussionist will act against your aunt tonight, eh?"

"Yes," I said. "He'd like to prove Warren's behind it, but if he can't prove anything, he won't arrest him. Also, he's all ready to provide funeral services for Aunt Lavinia. First-class. That way he'll make money out of it and won't lose face no matter what happens. Bonnefoi's terribly insecure but he's no fool."

"Funeral services!" said Timberline. "I thought he was a policeman."

As I was explaining the droll concession system practiced by the island's higher functionaries, Lord Bobby suddenly glanced at his watch, stood up, unplanted his swagger stick and, snapping it shut, said:

"I'm afraid I must leave at once. The glass-bottom boat departs in fifteen minutes and I must escort the ladies. I suggest we meet again before the voodoo show and escort Mrs. Vigorex in a group. Safety in numbers, you know. Above all, we've got to keep our wits about us—*and watch out for the drummer!*" He continued to look at us intently for a moment, then left. Just like that.

THE CARIBE

COCKTAIL

---

704. DIFFICULTY.—pinch, pretty pass, stress, brunt; critical situation, crisis; trial, rub, emergency, exigency, scramble.

scrape, hot water, hornet's nest; sea –, peck- of troubles; pretty kettle of fish; pickle, stew, *imbroglio,* mess.

At six o'clock, I was on the terrace of our cottage, martini in hand, waiting for Aunt Lavinia. The wind was up and the birds were going mad in the slashing, stroboscopic palm tops; sounds of preparatory activity down at the hotel. Mrs. Quigley arrived with Lord Bobby. Then Timberline. Aunt Lavinia came out. I mixed drinks. Lord Bobby, I noticed for the first time, bore a certain resemblance to Uncle Seward. He was as attentive to the ladies as at lunch but now he was watchful, glancing often at the gardens around us and taking care to occupy a chair on Aunt Lavinia's exposed flank. Mrs. Quigley looked apprehensive.

At six-thirty we started for the hotel terrace and the entertainment—Lord Bobby and I falling in close on either side of my aunt. We reached the hotel without incident. Most of the other guests were already at their tables with the pink umbrellas, having cocktails. Out on the terrace, the young woman of Warren's troupe was arranging a strange sort of altar made of stacked-up wooden boxes covered with rough cloth and decked with candles in bottles, gourds, hagiographical pictures and some other paraphernalia including a knife. Near by, the three tall cigar-butt-shaped drums were set up. To our left: the lawn, the Grecian pavilion, wind-flecked sea, low sun sweeping the stone terrace and boring, on our right, into the open glass doors of the hotel's main room. Warren and the rest of the troupe were in there waiting. (The manager kept appearing behind them and disappearing again.) Behind us: the darkening gardens; ahead: the front wing of the hotel and part of the palm-lined horseshoe drive approaching the entrance on the other side. Lord Bobby and I scanned the gardens and our glances met behind Aunt Lavinia.

Where were Bonnefoi and his merry men, I wondered? Were they cleverly concealed in the gardens and in the hotel ready to spring forth the moment the drummer made his move? Probably not. More likely they were roughhousing somewhere or enjoying themselves at Mama Tia's. No sign of any Boom-boom jeeps.

Sally came out of the doors of the hotel and went to the center of the terrace by the makeshift altar and faced the audience. She was wearing a simple black dress, no jewelry, and her look strayed over us a moment before she began a set speech about the ceremony we were about to see.

The loa to be summoned was Domballa, she told us, and explained the order of business: the chants and dancing, the drawing of the verver or symbolic design on the ground in front of the altar, the ritual offerings to the loa

(I glanced at Mrs. Quigley, who had turned pale under her powder), and finally—should the loa make an appearance—the possession of one or more of the congregation and the intervention of the houngan to release the possessed ones from the hold of the spirit. Then she went over to a table near the doors and sat down.

The other participants now filed out and joined the young woman, who was redistributing objects on the altar to keep the cloth from blowing. It was the same line-up as in San Francisco except for the addition of three young girls in red dresses and three more in white. The drummer came out last. Lord Bobby and I watched him as he took his place behind the drums and started a slow, heavy, intricate beat; as in San Francisco, he was staring over the heads of the audience as if he was seeing dark powers. Warren had sat down at the table with Sally. Timberline was watching Sally. The manager came out for a moment, looked around and then went back inside.

The sun was just going down now and the colors were brilliant everywhere—except that the faces of the performers were, as before, whitened and looked ghostly and unnatural. There was a smell of something like camellias and aromatic burning wood shifting in the wind. The other young man (besides the drummer) was evidently the acting houngan that night and was moving among the rest with odd little strutting steps, undulating his stomach muscles, and advancing with a slight pecking movement; occasionally, he would stop and pour some rum from a bottle on the altar around the wildly flickering candles. The old woman, Mama Céline, was swaying grimly in place, while the others (except the drummer) shifted about and turned in different directions to the quickening drums. They were chanting and the only words I could catch named the loa they were coaxing forth

> Domballa Ouedda!
> Domballa Oueddo!
> O - ay, o - ay, o - ay!

It does have an effect. After fifteen or twenty minutes of it, I suddenly realized that Mama Céline was not on the terrace any more. Shill was looking at me from her table. Lord Bobby glanced around rapidly as if he too had been caught off guard. Then we both turned our attention to the drummer, who just then raised his head—except it wasn't the same drummer! At some point in the hallucinatory shifting and chanting, the old man of the troupe had taken his place. Then the old man abruptly stopped drumming and behind us we heard a startling female cry and we all turned and discovered Mama Céline leading a black billy goat, with lighted candles affixed to its horns and harness, down the path from the gardens. The rest of the troupe responded in chorus, swaying more or less together, the drum took up again with a faster beat, heavily accented. As Mama Céline led the goat onto the terrace, through the chanting assembly and up to the altar, Lord Bobby and I looked around for the missing drummer. We spotted him together. He was crouching in the shadows just off the path behind us, about twenty yards from Aunt

Lavinia, raising a blowgun to his lips. I stood up and placed myself in the line of fire. Providentially Mrs. Quigley chose this moment to become afflicted by the spectacle on the terrace (the houngan was raising the stubby knife over the goat) and said she felt faint and had to leave. At this, Lord Bobby suggested they all leave; Aunt Lavinia agreed readily; in another moment he was guiding the two ladies away from the table, keeping close to Aunt Lavinia on her right, and past Warren and Sally's table into the hotel. I saw Warren watch them go in, then signal to the drummer, who started back up the path. I understood then that Warren meant him to intercept the trio after they had left the hotel by the other door and were on their way to the cottages. I told Timberline to stay at the table and ran up the path after the drummer.

Ahead, I saw him. He was crouching near the intersection of the other path from the hotel. I stopped too. The problem was that there was no way to approach him except directly down the Chicago-lit path. Another few yards and he would certainly see me. The man had a blowgun. I was hesitating whether to shout a warning to Lord Bobby (whose voice I could now hear through the shrubbery) when I was badly startled by a "Hssst!" right behind me. The red-feathered boy was standing there.

"I show you how to get him," he whispered, pointing to the man.

"O.K.," I said. "How?"

"Two dollars," he told me.

"A dollar."

"Okay," he said, grinning. "Dollar fifty."

He turned and I followed him through a wall of growth and we emerged on a second, hidden path, parallel to the main one, evidently worn through by panhandlers preying on the guests. We went up about fifty yards until the boy stopped and pointed through to a place on the other path.

"There is him," whispered the boy. "You pay now."

"Later," I said.

"You got a gun?"

"No."

"Knife?"

"No."

"You pay now."

"Later," I said again. He hesitated a second or two, then ran back down the hidden path. I moved through the brush cautiously, my steps covered by the birds and the chanting and drumming from the terrace. The drummer was crouched on my side of the path, blowgun across his knees. Now I could hear Aunt Lavinia's voice and then Mrs. Quigley's as they approached. The drummer started to raise his blowgun. I jumped.

Now, fortunately, there was a time in my early youth, when our ephemeral household was still intact, when I attended along with a half-dozen other refugees from nice families a course in body-building, self-defense and Confidence given in a musty gym on Union Street by a Mr. Gustafson. Thursdays from four to six. (I remember it always seemed to rain on Thursdays from four to six.) We learned wrestling, boxing and jujitsu and there in the gardens I attempted to apply all three of these manly disciplines against the drummer simultaneously.

Something must have worked, however, because after the initial impact of our bodies, I found that I had quietly and efficiently flattened him on his stomach and had him in a half-Nelson and was sitting on his back. My mistake was elementary. I put my free hand over his mouth to keep him quiet. He bit it. However, he made no sound as the other three passed quite close to us on the upper path.

When they had gone, I sat there thinking about what to do next. My captive was breathing more or less regularly now and was obstinately mute. He put up no resistance but I had the definite impression that he was only waiting for me to relax my hold for him to clobber me. Drummers have powerful arms. So I just sat there on him. After a while, I asked him if he spoke French. He just grunted something. It was already dark and as we were shadowed by bushes from the light of the outdoor fixture nearest us, I couldn't see his face, but then I asked myself what difference it really made whether we could communicate or not. How could I negotiate with someone when I was sitting on his back? How, for instance, could I ever believe the statements he might make? His very silence seemed to indicate that he too felt there could be no meaningful relationship between us. On the other hand, I couldn't very well get off him so I kept on sitting on him. Up the hill through the trees, I saw lights go on in Lord Bobby's cottage. Ours was still dark. They had all gone on up to Lord Bobby's.

Three or four minutes later, Timberline came up the path. She didn't see me at first and I called to her.

"Where are you?" she said.

"Over here."

"Did the man get away?"

"No," I said. "I'm sitting on him."

She came up and looked.

"That's Philippe," she said. The drummer looked up at her but continued to say nothing. "Sally told me about him. He's hypnotized."

"Sally?"

I listened as Timberline explained how Sally had come over to her table just after I had run up the path and sat with her and told her that Warren had drugged and hypnotized the drummer and ordered him to kill Aunt Lavinia with the blowgun that was now lying in the middle of the path. Surprisingly, the girls had gotten on beautifully.

"Captain Bonnefoi's down there too," she told me. "You should see him—he just arrived in a hearse with some other men and he's all dressed up in a top hat. The manager's trying to get him to leave."

"A hearse," I said. "He's crazy." (In the jeep that morning, Bonnefoi had told me about his hearse. He was very proud of it and had wanted to take me to see it at the garage where it was kept. He explained that Mama Tia wouldn't let him park it at her place on the theory that its presence was anti-erogenous. It had a new muffler but it needed an air filter, the original one having been lost or stolen, and Bonnefoi had asked me if I would send him an air filter for a 1957 Cadillac when I returned to the States. I had said I would see.)

The chants and drumming were frantic now. Timberline said:

"Your friend Warren seems to think Bonnefoi's men will be up here any minute to get your aunt. He thinks Philippe has already killed her. That's what Sally says."

"Warren is crazy too," I said. I was trying to think.

"So why don't we tell Captain Bonnefoi to have them come up?"

"Who?"

"The men who came with him with the hearse and the coffin."

"Timberline!" I said, astonished. "Aunt Lavinia's up at Lord Bobby's cottage. She's perfectly all right—and she will be as long as I'm sitting on Philippe."

Hearing his name, Philippe made a sudden effort to free himself but I managed to hold him pinned.

"Of course," said Timberline, "but Warren doesn't know that, does he? And Sally said he'd be coming up to find you—afterwards."

We could see each other in the darkness now. Suddenly I got the message.

"Get Bonnefoi up here," I said. "Tell him to bring someone with him to take care of Philippe. Tell him if he plays ball there's money in it for him. And incidentally—you're marvelous." She smiled but didn't move at first.

"Avery."

"What?"

"Nothing." She started to turn down the path.

"Timberline."

"Yes?"

"I haven't had a chance to ask you before—but will you marry me?"

When she said yes, I almost forgot about the drummer.

As Bonnefoi's corporal (think of the Michelin stacked-up-tire man) marched Philippe off at the end of an imaginary line extending from the muzzle of his revolver, Bonnefoi and I negotiated. At first he was reluctant. His own thought, of course, had been to let the drummer go. But when I agreed to pay for the funeral services just as if Aunt Lavinia was actually benefiting from them, in dollars, and added certain fringe benefits to the proposition, he finally agreed to co-operate. I was to supply four bottles of rum for the croquemorts and a bottle of White Horse for Bonnefoi personally; I was also to make every effort when I was back in San Francisco to see that Bonnefoi's name appeared in the *Chronicle*. (This last offer was a sheer hunch, but judging by Bonnefoi's reaction it was the crucial talking point.)

So Bonnefoi went down to organize the funeral detail and Timberline and I went up to our cottage where we kissed and parted, she to Lord Bobby's to try to keep Aunt Lavinia up there and I up on the terrace to await Bonnefoi and (if what Sally had said proved to be true) Warren.

Five minutes later, I spotted Bonnefoi's top hat through

the trees and then the entire party: Bonnefoi leading four of his policemen, now wearing black suits, carrying the coffin, which was covered with a large American flag. They were chanting a sort of voodoo requiem and I realized then that the drums on the hotel terrace were beating out a slow march and the celebrants were silent. I stepped back out of sight and watched the four set the coffin on the ground, Bonnefoi issuing crisp orders and doing it all very smartly. The men stood at attention until his back was turned; then, as he started up the stairs, three of them began making violent lunges at each other's flies, while the fourth, aloof from this amusement, stretched out on top of the coffin with a bottle.

"First-class," said Bonnefoi to me, not having observed the insubordination. We had a drink. Then from the terrace he got his unruly men mustered, and we watched the coffin jogging unsteadily back down the path. Meanwhile, the ceremony had entered a final phase in which it seemed that Domballa and any other spirits accidentally fetched were being sung off to their habitations with glorias and hosannas.

Then the drums took up the dirge beat.

Bonnefoi's Black Maria looked rather fine going down the drive and out the gates.

Warren appeared only moments after Bonnefoi had managed to squeeze himself into Aunt Lavinia's clothes closet. I was sitting in the living room. He stood in the doorway from the terrace a moment, then came in and sat in an armchair opposite me.

"That wasn't smart of you to go up in the gardens that way," he said. "After all our carefully laid plans, that could weaken your alibi. Besides, Philippe might have killed you."

"Well, he didn't," I said. "He killed Aunt Lavinia."

"Of course. How does it feel to be a very wealthy man?"

"All right, I guess. Sort of soon to tell."

He settled back in the chair and pulled out a package of Kents. "Yes," he said, grinning now, "probate does take a while—probably more than a year with an estate like that, but in the meantime your credit's good as gold. Also perhaps Shag can speed things along for us. I always say that whenever they really want to, lawyers can—"

"Us?"

"Certainly. Oh, your obligation to Shag is an affair between you and him now—he'll have time to think about it during the probate, won't he? But" (he looked at his watch) "as for Aunt June, her never-very-useful existence will be terminated in about five and a half hours, allowing for the time difference."

"You mean Shag—"

"The Bat Burglar. His *second* visit."

He watched me for a moment over the flame of his lighter, then lit his cigarette.

"You see," he went on, "I sort of figured you two might try the obvious thing—that's why I cleaned up the house immediately. Then when Aunt June told me about her little fright— But don't worry, this time our friend is very thoroughly prepared. I don't know what went wrong with you when I suggested you go to Mrs. Peabody, but it won't happen with Shag. Think of it, he's more than three thousand miles away, and in a little while he'll be doing exactly what I've already suggested he do. Exactly. Isn't it amazing?"

"Could you stop him if you wanted to?"

"Yes. I could. That is, if the phones on this rotten island were working, which wouldn't be very likely. I could. But you couldn't. Nobody else could. Nobody else would get through to him. The suggestion is very deeply implanted, far below the conscious level. Notice I say suggestion—but he'll take it as an absolute order."

I couldn't think of anything constructive to say just then, and Warren continued in his unbearably smug manner:

"After the formalities in San Francisco, I'm never coming back to this pesthole—" There was a clacking sound in the closet in my aunt's room; Bonnefoi must have touched a coat hanger, but Warren was too absorbed in what he was saying to notice. "I've had it here with these people," he was saying. "I've learned a lot of things from them, very useful things too, some of them, but now there's no sense to it. I won't have to live here with these blacks any more because you know in the end, Avery, whatever you say, you want to be with your own people. After the funeral and estate formalities, I'm going to settle in the States. I have friends, Avery, powerful friends, people of great wealth and—strong principles, men who are accustomed to having their way, one way or the other. I've had this island. Have you seen the President? No, of course you haven't, he hardly ever dares step out of his palace these days. He's a lunatic, you know. A great meat-eater. He listens to no one but the loas and me and the day is approaching when he'll stop listening to me—that's what that homicidal idiot Bonnefoi is waiting for; he's just waiting around for the President to stop listening to me and then —But I'm not staying around for that. I'm leaving today and I'm taking a little souvenir with me: a hundred and fifty thousand dollars. Yes. It's from the casino and I figure this country owes me at least that for services rendered. Of course I'm taking my—documents too, including our own agreement, and of course my personal mementos from the old days at Casita. They mean a lot to me, Avery, those days. I don't know whether you understand that." His face went solemn, then he grinned again. "What would Fogg say to a suitcase with a hundred and fifty thousand dollars in it? I haven't done quite so badly as he used to predict, have I? As a matter of fact, I've been thinking of sending the School a little contribution, say of ten thousand dollars. What would Fogg say to that?"

"Is Sally going with you?" I asked loudly and quickly to cover a rustle from the closet where Bonnefoi was.

"No," he said slowly. "Sally isn't. Lately, she's not been everything I have to expect in an assistant. Especially lately. By the way, I notice you seem to be quite taken with her."

"Just friendly."

"Well, don't get too friendly—for your own sake. Anyway, I'm not sure she'd fit in very well now, so she's staying back." Again he looked at his watch and seemed to be on the point of leaving. "There's a Learjet at the airport for me right now. We have plans, Avery, patriotic enterprises. I can tell you it will be a considerable relief to be working with white people again."

It was quite impressive the way Bonnefoi came through the fragile louvered doors. One side he took off altogether, the other was half off its hinges and slammed back against the wall. Bonnefoi stood there in the bedroom doorway, breathing heavily, his booted legs planted wide apart, holding a trembling revolver in his two hands and obviously upset. I saw Warren turn pale, but, to his credit, his lemony grin was still in place when the lights dimmed, wavered and went out.

Bonnefoi took half the living-room furniture with him as he made for the terrace, but Warren was probably halfway to the hotel by the time the police captain was down the terrace step in pursuit. When he had gone, I noticed a cigarette glow bright in one of the wicker chairs.

"Timberline?"

"Try again."

"Shill," I said. "I mean Sally."

"Yes," she said. "Sally."

I went over and sat down next to her.

"Listen, who are you for," I blurted out, "him or me?"

I could just make out she was smiling when she said, "Not for him."

"You gave him back the Contract."

"Yes," she said, "but I still wasn't sure of myself then. But I am now—thanks in part to you, Mr. Frog."

After a moment I said (rather unnecessarily as I knew

she'd seen and heard it all), "Warren got away in the Blackout."

"I know. I wouldn't worry about it."

"Aren't you? He seems sort of annoyed with you."

"I know. But I'm not worrying about it."

Down at the hotel, I heard Warren's Porsche start up, heard the tires squeal and got up to watch its lights sweep down the horseshoe drive. I heard Bonnefoi yelling. Other headlights, outside the gates, came on Warren's car as it shot out into the roadway. The hearse roared flat-out up the drive, pitched forward to a stop at the hotel entrance; Bonnefoi got in, issuing commands; the hearse blasted air-filterlessly down the drive again and out the gates. Sally was standing beside me.

"They'll never catch him in that thing," I said. "He's got a plane waiting for him at the airport."

"I know," she said again, quietly. The cottage windows shuddered slightly.

"What was that?" I asked.

"That was Warren."

"What happened to him?"

She sent her cigarette over-ending into the gardens.

"I guess he must have shifted into fourth gear."

The bomb, she told me, had been made from one of the Army-rejected mortar rounds Warren had been supplying Hermosa's forces but it had apparently worked well enough. Sally had found the thing in her car after Ozo had warned her Warren had had him put it there. Some time after her brief talk with Timberline, Sally, using her C.I.A. know-how, had personally put the device in Warren's car so that it was triggered by the transmission linkage.

"But why did he want to kill you?" I said, rather awed.

"Oh, like they say, I knew an awful lot. Also, you heard him say I wouldn't fit in any more. I agree with him there." The glazed Shill look had crept back into her eyes, but then she seemed to be fighting free of something. "You see, when I first met you in San Francisco, I was only about half there. I was Warren's best subject. His prize guinea pig. He tried everything on me." She thought a moment, then added, "I mean he tried everything. He wanted to prove his theories about mind control—different combinations of drugs and deep hypnosis and disassociative stuff and—" She hesitated.

"Go on," I said.

"But that was only part of what he wanted to prove. Mostly he wanted to prove himself. As a man. As a human being. Only he couldn't ever do that, that was what was wrong."

"You mean he couldn't—"

"Oh, sure—technically. Mechanically Warren was all there. But there wasn't any love in him or any human feeling at all. It was like he was born blind or something." She paused again, then: "The only thing that was even *like* human involvement for him was that crazy school experience you all had—that's why he had to go through with your Contract." We heard laughter from Lord Bobby's cottage. "He had to keep that alive. You see, intimidating people and controlling them and killing them was what Warren did instead of loving anybody." Then she dropped back to the earlier topic: "Oh, Warren *that way* was as safe as they come. You can't *really* get hurt by somebody like that."

"Warren was—safe?"

"For a girl, completely. All monsters are safe."

"But he almost killed you. He put a real bomb in your car."

"I didn't say you couldn't get killed. I said you couldn't get hurt."

As I was pondering this, she slipped something into my inside jacket pocket, then patted the pocket.

"The Contract?"

"Souvenir," she said.

With a flood of relief, I thought: Aunt Lavinia is out of danger and I'm free again. Then I had another thought: Shag!

The Blackout ended just as Lord Bobby and the three ladies with him came up the terrace steps. By great luck I found the phone was working too; it crackled, beeped, hummed as if the island's loas were on the line, but the international operator was putting me through to San Francisco. Lord Bobby came into the bedroom as the others settled on the terrace. (Mrs. Quigley was asking nervously, "But who is Avery telephoning?" and "But what was it we heard? Does anyone know anything?")

"He's dead," I whispered to Lord Bobby, covering the

phone. "A bomb." He closed his eyes for an instant, his massive Britannic features tensely set.

"Bonnefoi?" he asked me.

"Sally."

The phone was ringing Shag's home number. Lord Bobby went back out on the terrace.

"Hello."

"Hi, Shag."

"Hi, Ave. How's everything?" His voice sounded oddly dull.

"Warren's dead," I said, "and I have the Contract back."
Silence.

"Did you hear me?"

"Yes. Warren's dead and you have the Contract back."

"So everything's all right now."

"Yes. Everything's all right now." Pause. "How's everything?"

"Shag, listen—what are you doing tonight? I mean right now."

"Nothing." Pause. "I'm going out." Heavy petulance had entered his voice.

"Shag," I said urgently, "Warren has hypnotized you. He's given you a post-hypnotic suggestion to kill his aunt tonight. Can you hear me?"

There was a long silence, then bleeps and maritime noises like crabs eating at the cable, then:

"I can hear you. So long, Ave."

Sally was there, taking the phone out of my hand.

"Shag," she said, "this is Shill. Remember?" There was a reluctant crackle in the receiver. "Remember what

Warren told you that afternoon? He told you to go to Mrs. Oliphant's tonight. Remember about going up the stairs? You had to be careful of a certain stair because it creaked. Which stair, Shag?"

She held the phone so I could hear it. Again there was a series of faint bleeps, then Shag's voice:

"The seventh. I'll remember."

Then he hung up.

Timberline came in from the terrace. It was her idea that we call Mrs. Peabody.

"Well," said Aunt Lavinia when we were all out on the terrace together, "it has been an exciting day—the glass-bottom boat was thrilling, and of course the voodoo show, and then we even had a Blackout. Lord Bobby, you must visit us in San Francisco as soon as possible."

"How kind," murmured Lord Bobby, "how very kind."

"Tomorrow Avery and Kee-kee and I will be returning. I think we've had enough adventure for a while. Haven't we, Avery?" Timberline smiled, only it wasn't really a smile, it just looked like one.

I said: "Aunt Lavinia, I won't be staying in San Francisco. I'm going to New York. Miss St. Denis and I are getting married."

Sometimes Aunt Lavinia can surprise you and this was one of the times. Her immortal words were: "Well, how very nice. Congratulations, Avery."

Then everyone else was congratulating us; Sally went

over and embraced Timberline; and none of us noticed that our waiter was standing at the head of the terrace stairs with a tray of rum punches Lord Bobby had ordered. When he saw Aunt Lavinia, the glasses started tinkling together like temple bells.

"What in the world was the matter with that man?" asked Aunt Lavinia when the waiter had served the drinks and hurriedly left. "Did you see the way he was looking at me?"

Ten minutes later, the phone rang. I answered it. It was Mrs. Peabody assuring me that she had reached Shag in time and that everything was all right and that she was going to bed.

"Now what *exactly* have you young people been up to in the past hour?" demanded Lord Bobby, when we had left Aunt Lavinia and Mrs. Quigley and settled at a table in the hotel bar. "I have a feeling I've been missing out on all the fun."

We told him. As we talked, the manager, sitting at a small table working on an account book, watched us more and more uncomfortably. Finally, he got up and came over and said to me, "Mr. Ashley, your aunt— The 'earse—"

"*H*earse," corrected Lord Bobby, pounding his chest to show where the *h* came from.

"Oh yes," I said, "I wanted to speak to you about that. You could have given my aunt a nasty shock, you know?"

"I? Monsieur! But Captain Bonnefoi told me she was— dead!"

We all looked at each other.

"Dead? Not at all," said Lord Bobby finally, then looked at me. "Fact is, I thought she was looking particularly fit this evening. Didn't you?"

"Now," went on Lord Bobby matter-of-factly as we watched the manager returning to his little table, "let's see if I have it all straight: Sally switched the bomb from her car into Oliphant's—"

"And Avery sat on the drummer—" said Timberline.

"And Timberline thought of making Warren think Aunt Lavinia was dead—" I said.

"And you got Mrs. Vigorex away from the table just in time," said Sally to Lord Bobby.

"Yes—thanks to Mrs. Quigley's indisposition. But of course—I'm ineligible."

"For what?" the three of us asked at once.

"Oh, didn't I mention it?" said Lord Bobby uncandidly. "There's a reward put up by some of us at the Peregrine Society for the conviction or—liquidation of Thackery Baxter's murderer. A thousand guineas, as a matter of fact. You see, we all thought very highly of poor Baxter, very highly."

Then, as Lord Bobby explained for Sally's benefit his mission to Saint Sebastian to avenge the death of the late clubman, he pulled out a checkbook and a pen. He wrote three checks. As he did, the little red-feathered boy managed to slip into the bar area unobserved and stood beside me with his hand out for the dollar fifty.

286

EPILOGUE

67. END.—*N.* end, close, termination; disinence, conclusion, *finis, finale,* period, term, *terminus,* last, *omega;* ex-treme, -tremity; gable –, butt –, fag-end; tip, nib, point; tail &c. (*rear*) 235; verge &c. (*edge*) 231; tag, peroration; *bonne bouche.*

consummation, *dénouement;* finish &c. (*completion*)

I AM writing this somewhere over an incandescent spider web Captain Marshall says is Denver. Our stewardess for the flight is Miss Ort. Just two hours ago, the plane's door clumped shut on the San Francisco International Airport and my last vision of Aunt Lavinia waving Kee-kee's indifferent paw to me from behind the terminal glass. Witter was standing beside her. Then the take-off absorbed me (as take-offs always do) in the awesome farce of mortality and the remarkable elasticity of metal under stress.

Now, up here in the comparative security of the sub-stratosphere over Denver, I pen this postscript to the Contract adventure with an odd, slightly queasy sense of being suspended, like a ball in the air, between two phases in my life. For some reason, I find myself thinking back twenty years to a lunch-time in the playground at the Ulysses S. Grant School when a boy called Sonny Blumegarden —our Zoroaster, our prophet of the Atomic Age—expounded the Fourth Dimension to us as we ate our sandwiches. I can still see his narrow face, dark and puckered with knowledge, as he bent over his macerated Eberhard and drew inside the cover of his arithmetic book two cubes, one within the other like Chinese boxes, then connected the corners and said, "That's *time*, dumbbells. That's what the Fourth Dimension is." He smelled of cleaning fluid and there was a gob of French's Prepared Mustard on his cords.

That, if I remember, was the year my parental home, so to speak, floated out into the Pacific and I went to live with Aunt Lavinia on Washington Street. The next year: Casita Encantada.

Aunt Lavinia is home again now, probably receiving her guests. She is having a few people for dinner: the Princess, Witter, Mrs. Bush, I believe, Mrs. Quigley, Freddie, and a visiting Spanish count currently being lionized by the dowagers of San Francisco. There has been no more than the usual run of disturbance in the neighborhood: a bomb in the Yugoslavian consulate, a mother of seven struck in the foot by a sniper's bullet, a jewel theft attributed to the Bat Burglar (Inspector Ferguson promises an early arrest). In the week I have been back winding up my affairs (closing my bank account, shipping personal effects, selling my car), I have seen Shag a couple of times but we have been strangely guarded with each other in discussing the recent events. Shag seems to be more than ever plunged into estate and trust work, Chamber of Commerce meetings, cocktail parties, sports and group singing. He has hinted, in an exploratory way, that there might be wedding bells ahead for him and Patricia Bunson. I have assured him that he has my blessing and that I wish them every happiness.

In less than three hours, Timberline will be meeting me at LaGuardia Airport. She writes that she has found a two-and-a-half-room apartment in a part of New York called the East Village, not far from her parents' warehouse. The rent is $130, which seems high for a two-and-a-half-room apartment, but apparently rents are higher in New York. My share of the Peregrine Society money should tide us over until I find a job.

Also in my pocket is a letter from Sally. She has matriculated again at the University of Michigan but meanwhile has met someone who works in the Synthetics Division of the Monsanto Chemical Corporation, and from the way she writes I wouldn't be surprised if she soon became Mrs. Warren Diebenmacher. I can't quite see Sally as an ordinary suburban housewife with children and everything but I suppose stranger things have happened.

Aunt June, I assume, still sits in the haze of her TV, taking it all in. With Warren's death, everything will now go to the Theosophical Society, Shag says, and I like to think that some day, if only theosophically, she will finally have her long-awaited experience in the underworld.

Strangest of all is the change in Mrs. Peabody's life. Though still in remarkably sound health, she has lately decided that she will no longer receive people or pay calls, attend functions (even the Symphony), or even speak on the telephone. There is a female companion with her now, as well as her Henry, and she still goes out almost every afternoon in the Armstrong-Sidley, sometimes leaving messages and presents or books she wants people to read at her friends' houses, but she stays in the car. No one can explain why she has chosen to cut herself off from her world so completely. Shag says she told him in their last phone communication that she had decided she had had enough stimulation for one life.

I was as good as my word to Bonnefoi. Connie's piece in last Tuesday's Society page ran in part:

> "VOODOO A-GO-GO
> At home after a Caribe sojourn at the oh-so-posh Paradise Roc Beach Club on once-popping now popular Saint Sebastian: Mrs. Seward ("Livvy") Vigorex and Mrs. Howard Quigley. While junketing the San Franciscans were hosted by Lord Robert ("Bobby") Twitchell, over from London for the voodoo. Both vet globe-trotters had high praise for Saint Sebastian officialdom, especially the personable Police Chief Jean Bonnefoi ..."

(On the phone: "I didn't say anything about any personable officials, did you? You didn't? Well, I just don't know what gets into Connie Beasy!")

Ozo is on my mind. Perhaps some day I will return to Saint Sebastian and redeem the promise Sally made so inconsiderately in my name; but in the meantime, Ozo will just have to get along the best he can, like everybody else.